PATTY AND AZALEA

CAROLYN WELLS

1st WORLD
LIBRARY
Literary Society

Patty and Azalea

Carolyn Wells

© 1st World Library, 2006
PO Box 2211
Fairfield, IA 52556
www.1stworldlibrary.com
First Edition

LCCN: 2006937739

Softcover ISBN: 978-1-4218-3320-0
Hardcover ISBN: 978-1-4218-3220-3
eBook ISBN: 978-1-4218-3420-7

Purchase *"Patty and Azalea"*
as a traditional bound book at:
www.1stWorldLibrary.com/purchase.asp?ISBN=978-1-4218-3320-0

1st World Library is a literary, educational organization
dedicated to:

- Creating a free internet library of downloadable ebooks

- Hosting writing competitions and offering book
publishing scholarships.

Interested in more 1st World Library books?
contact: literacy@1stworldlibrary.com
Check us out at: www.1stworldlibrary.com

1st World Library Literary Society

Giving Back to the World

"If you want to work on the core problem, it's early school literacy."

- James Barksdale, former CEO of Netscape

"No skill is more crucial to the future of a child, or to a democratic and prosperous society, than literacy."

- Los Angeles Times

Literacy... means far more than learning how to read and write... The aim is to transmit... knowledge and promote social participation."

- UNESCO

"Literacy is not a luxury, it is a right and a responsibility. If our world is to meet the challenges of the twenty-first century we must harness the energy and creativity of all our citizens."

- President Bill Clinton

"Parents should be encouraged to read to their children, and teachers should be equipped with all available techniques for teaching literacy, so the varying needs and capacities of individual kids can be taken into account."

- Hugh Mackay

THIS BOOK IS DEDICATED WITH LOVING GOOD
WISHES TO PRISCILLA KERLEY

CONTENTS

I. WISTARIA PORCH 7

II. GUESTS ARRIVE.. 19

III. BETTY GALE 31

IV. A NEW RELATIVE.. 43

V. THAT AWFUL AZALEA...................................... 55

VI. TABLE MANNERS 67

VII. MYSTERIOUS CALLERS.................................. 79

VIII. MISSING 92

IX. VANITY FAIR 104

X. INQUIRIES.. 117

XI. THE SAMPLER... 128

XII. AZALEA'S CHANCE... 140

XIII. "STAR OF THE WEST".................................... 152

XIV. AT THE PICTURE PLAY 164

XV. SOME RECORDS... 176

XVI. AZALEA'S STORY... 188

XVII. PHILIP'S REQUEST 200

XVIII. PHILIP'S BROWNIE.................................... 213

CHAPTER I

WISTARIA PORCH

"Oh, Little Billee! Come quick, for goodness' sake! The baby's choking!"

Patty was in the sun parlour, her arms full of a fluttering bundle of lace and linen, and her blue eyes wide with dismay at her small daughter's facial contortions.

"Only with laughter," Bill reassured her after a quick glance at the restless infant. "Give her to me."

The baby nestled comfortably in his big, powerful arms, and Patty sat back in her chair and watched them both.

"What a pleasure," she said, complacently, "to be wife and mother to two such fine specimens of humanity! She grows more and more like you every day, Little Billee."

"Well, if this yellow fuzz of a head and this pinky peach of a face is like anybody in the world except Patty Farnsworth, I'll give up! Why, she's the image of you,—except when she makes these grotesque grimaces,—like a Chinese Joss."

"Stop it! You shan't call my baby names! She's a booful-poofle! She's a hunny-bunny! She's her mudder's pressus girly-wirly, —so she wuz!"

"Oh, Patty, that I should live to hear you talk such lingo! I thought you were going to be sensible."

"How can anybody be sensible with a baby like that! Isn't she the very wonderfullest ever! Oh, Billee, look at her angel smile!"

"Angel smile? More like a mountebank's grin! But I'm sure she means well. And I'll agree she is the most wonderful thing in the world."

Bill tossed the child up and down, and chuckled at her evident appreciation of his efforts for her amusement.

"Be careful of my baby, if you please," and Patty eyed the performance dubiously. "Suppose you drop my child?"

"I hardly think I shall, ma'am. And, incidentally, I suppose she is my child?"

"No; a girl baby is always her mudder's own—only just her very own mudder's own. Give her to me! Let me has my baby,—my ownty-donty baby!"

Farnsworth obediently handed Patty her property, and put another pillow behind her as she sat in the low willow chair. Then he seated himself near, and adoringly watched his two treasures.

It was mid-April and the Farnsworths had been married more than a year. On their return from France, they had looked about for a home, and had at last found a fortunate chance to buy at a bargain a beautiful place up in Westchester County. It was near enough to New York for a quick trip and yet it was almost country.

The small settlement of Arden was largely composed of fine estates and attractive homes. This one which they had taken was broad and extensive, with hundreds of acres in lawns, gardens and woodland. It was called Wistaria Porch, because of an old wistaria vine which had achieved astounding dimensions and whose blooms in the spring and foliage later were the admiration of the whole countryside.

The house itself was modern and of the best Colonial design. Indeed, it was copied in nearly every detail from the finest type of Colonial mansion. Though really too large for such a small family, both Patty and Bill liked spacious rooms and lots of them, so they decided to take it, and shut off such parts as they didn't need. But no rooms were shut off, and they revelled in a great library beside their living-room and drawing-room. They had a cosy breakfast room beside the big dining-room and there were a music room and a billiard room and a den and great hall with a spreading staircase; and the second story was a maze of bedrooms, guest rooms and bathrooms.

It took Patty some days even to learn her way round, and she loved every room, hall and passage. There were fascinating windows, great wide and deep ones, and little oriels and dormers. There were unexpected turns and nooks, and there was,—which brought joy to Patty's heart,—plenty of closet space.

The whole place was of noble proportions and magnificent size, but Patty's home-making talents brought cosiness to the rooms they themselves used and stateliness and beauty to the more formal apartments.

"We must look ahead," she told Billee, "for I expect to spend my whole life here. I don't want to fix a place up just as I like it, and then scoot off and leave it and live somewhere else. And when our daughter begins to have beaux and entertain house parties, we'll need all the room there is."

"You have what Mr. Lucas calls a 'leaping mind,'" Bill remarked. "But I'm ready to confess I like room enough to swing a cat in,—even if I've no intention of swinging poor puss."

And so they set blithely to work to furnish their ancestral halls, as Patty called them, claiming that an ancestral hall had to have a beginning some time, and she was beginning hers now.

Such fun as it was selecting rugs and hangings, furniture and ornaments, books and pictures.

Lots of things they had bought abroad, for Captain Bill had been fortunate in his affairs and had had some leisure time in France and England after the war was over to collect some art treasures.

Also, they didn't try or want to complete the whole house at once. Part of the fun would be in adding bits later on, and if there were no place to put them, there would be no fun in buying things.

Patty was a wise and careful buyer. Only worth-while things were selected, not a miscellaneous collection of trumpery junk. So the result to date was charming furniture and appointments, but space for more when desired.

Little Billee's taste, too, was excellent, and he and Patty nearly always agreed on their choice. But it was a rule that if either disapproved, the thing in question was not bought. Only such as both sanctioned could come into their home.

The house had a wide and hospitable Colonial doorway, with broad fanlight above and columns at either side. Seats, too, flanked the porch, and the carefully trimmed wistaria vine hung gracefully over all. Across both ends of the house ran wide verandahs, with *porte cochere*, sun parlour, conservatory and tea-porch breaking the monotony.

Patty's own bedroom was an exquisite nest, done up in blue and silver, and her boudoir, opening from it, was a dream of pink and white. Then came the baby's quarters; the day nursery, gay with pictured walls and the sun porch, bright and airy.

Carolyn Wells

For the all-important baby was now two months old, and entitled to consideration as a real member of the family.

Fleurette was her name, only selected after long thought and much discussion. Bill had stood out for Patricia Fairfield Farnsworth, but Patty declared no child of hers should be saddled with such a burden for life! Then Bill declared it must be a diminutive, in some way, of the mother's name, and as he always called Patty his Blossom Girl, the only suggestion worth considering was something that meant Little Flower. And as their stay in France had made the French language seem less foreign than of yore, they finally chose Fleurette,—the Baby Blossom.

Farnsworth was a man of affairs, and had sometimes to go to Washington or other distant cities on business, but not often or for a long stay. And as Patty expressed it, that was a lot better than for him to have to go to New York every day,—as so many men of their acquaintance did.

"I never thought I'd be as happy as this," Patty said, as, still holding her baby, she sat rocking slowly, and gazing alternately at her husband and her child.

"Why not?" Farnsworth inquired, as he lighted a fresh cigar.

"Oh, it's too much for any one mortal! Here I've the biggest husband in the world, and the littlest baby—"

"Oh, come now,—that's no incubator chick!"

"No, she's fully normal size, Nurse says, but she's a tiny mite as yet," and Patty cuddled the mite in an ecstasy of maternal joy.

"I thought friend Nurse wouldn't let you snuggle the kiddy like that."

"She doesn't approve,—but she's still at her lunch and when

the cat's away—"

And then the white uniformed nurse appeared, and smiled at pretty Patty as she took the baby from her cuddling arms.

"Come for a ride, Patty *Maman*?" asked her husband, as they left the little Fleurette's presence.

"No; let's go for a walk. I want to look over the west glade, and see if it will stand a Japanese tea-house there."

"All right, come ahead. You've not forgotten your dinky tea-porch?"

"No; but this is different. A tea-house is lovely, and—"

"All right, Madame Butterfly, have one if you like. Come down this way."

They went along a picturesque path, between two rocky ravines,—a bit of real scenic effect that made, indeed, a fine setting for a little structure for a pleasure house of any kind.

"Lovely spot!" and Patty stood still and gazed about over her domain.

"Seems to me I've heard you remark that before."

"And will again,—so long as we both shall live! Oh, Little Billee, I'm so glad I picked you out for my mate—"

"*I* picked *you* out, you mean. Why, the first moment I saw you, I—"

"You kissed me! Yes, you did,—you bad man! I wonder I ever spoke to you again!"

"But I kissed you by mistake that time. I'd no idea who you were."

Carolyn Wells

"I know it. And you've no idea who I am, now!"

"That's true, sweetheart. For you've as many moods and personalities as a chameleon,—and each more dear and sweet than the last."

"Look here, my friend, haven't we been married long enough for you to cease to feel the necessity for those pretty speeches?"

"Tired of 'em?"

"No; but I don't want you to think you must—"

"Now, now, don't be Patty Simpleton! When I make forced or perfunctory speeches, you'll know it! Don't you think so, Patty Mine?"

"Yep. Oh, Billee, look, there's the place for the tea-house!"

Patty pointed to a shady nook, halfway up the side of the ravine.

"Great!" agreed Bill. "Wait a minute,—I'll sketch it in."

He pulled an old envelope and a pencil from his pockets, and rapidly drew the location with a few hasty strokes, and added a suggestion of an Oriental looking building that was meant for the proposed tea-house.

"Just right!" cried Patty; "you *are* clever, dear! Now draw Baby and me drinking tea there."

A few more marks did for the tea drinkers and a queer looking figure hurrying along the path was doubtless the father coming home.

Patty declared herself satisfied and folded the paper and put it safely away in her pocket.

"We'll get at that as soon as the landscape gardener finishes the sunken garden," she said.

"Oh, I'm *glad* I'm alive! I never expected to have everything I wanted in the way of gardens! Don't you love them, too?"

"Of course,—and yet, not as you do, Patty. I was brought up in the great West, you know,—and sometimes I long for the big spaces."

"Why, this is a big space, isn't it?"

"I mean the prairies,—yes, even the desert,—the limitless expanse of—"

"Limitless fiddlesticks! You can't have the earth!"

"I don't want it. You're all the world to me, then why crave the earth?"

"Nice boy! Well, as I was about to say, do you know, I think it's time we had some guests up here, just for to see and to admire this paradise of ours."

"Have them, by all means. Are you settled enough?"

"Oh, yes. And I shan't have anything much to do. Mrs. Chase is a host in herself, and Nurse Winnie takes full charge of my child,—with Susie's help."

"Do you own that infant exclusively, ma'am? I notice you always say *my* child!"

"As I've told you, you don't count. Why, you won't really count until the day when some nice young man comes to ask you for the hand of Mademoiselle Fleurette."

"Heaven forbid the day! I'll send him packing!"

"Indeed you won't! I want my daughter to marry and live happy ever after,—as *I'm* doing."

"Are you, Patty? Are you happy?"

As Billee asked this question a dozen times a day for the sheer joy of watching Patty's lovely face smile an affirmative, she didn't think it necessary to enlarge on the subject.

"I do be," she said, succinctly, and Farnsworth believed her.

"Now, I propose," she went on, "that we have a week-end house-party. That's the nicest way to show off the place—"

"Patty! Are you growing proud and ostentatious?"

"I'm proud—very much so, of my home and my family,—but nobody ever called me ostentatious! What *do* you mean?"

"Nothing. I spoke thoughtlessly. But you are puffed up with pride and vanity,—*I* think."

"Who wouldn't be—with all this?"

Patty swept an arm off toward the acres of their domain, and smiled happily in her delight of ownership.

"Well, anyway," she went on, "we'll ask Elise and Bumble and Phil and Kenneth and Chick and—"

"Don't get too many,—you'll wear yourself all out just talking to them."

"No: a big party entertain themselves better than a few. Well, I'll fix up the list. Anybody you want specially?"

"No, not now. Some time we'll have Mona and Roger, of course; and some time Daisy—"

"Yes, when we have Adele and Jim. Oh, won't we have lots of jolly parties! Thank goodness we've plenty of guest rooms."

"Are they all in order?"

"Not quite. I have to make lace things and fiddle-de-fads for some of them."

"Can't you buy those?"

"Some I do, but some I like to make. It's no trouble, and they're prettier."

"Let's go back around by the garage, I want to see Larry."

They strolled around through the well-kept vegetable gardens and chicken yards, and came to the garage. Here were the big cars and Patty's own little runabout. Larry, the chauffeur, touched his cap with a respectful smile at Patty, and as Farnsworth talked to the man, Patty stood looking off across the grounds and wondering if any one in the whole world loved a home as she did.

Then they went on, strolling by the flower beds and formal gardens.

"And through the land at eve they went," quoted Bill, softly.

"And on her lover's arm she leant," Patty took up the verse.

"And round her waist she felt it fold," continued he:

> "And far across the hills they went
> To that new world which is the old.
> And far across the dying day,
> Beyond its utmost purple rim:
> Beyond the night, across the day
> The happy Princess followed him."

"Through all the world she followed him," added Patty; "I think our quotations are a bit inaccurate, but we have the gist of Tennyson's ideas."

"And the gist is—?"

"That I'm a happy Princess," she smiled.

"Well, you're in your element, that's certain. I never saw anybody enjoy fixing up a house as you do!"

"Did you ever see anybody fix up a house, anyway?"

"I'm not sure I ever did. I had very little home life, dear."

"Well, you're going to make up for that now. You're going to have so much home life from now on, that you can hardly stagger under it. And I'm going to make it!"

"Then it will be a real true home-made home! Sometimes, Patty, I fear that with all your tea-houses and formal gardens you'll lose the real homey effect—"

"Lose your grandmother! Why, in the right hands, all those faddy things melt into one big bundle of hominess, and you feel as if you'd always had 'em. Soon you'll declare you've never lived without a Japanese tea-garden in your back yard!"

"I believe you! You'd make a home feeling in the Parthenon, —if you chose to live there!"

"Of course I should! Or in the Coliseum, or in the Taj Mahal."

"There, there, that will do! Don't carry your vaunts further! Now come around the house, and let's go in under the wistaria. It's a purple glory now!"

"So it is! What a stunning old vine it is. I did think I'd change the name of the place, but that wistaria over that porch is too fine to be discarded. Let's get Mr. Hepworth up here to paint it."

"It must be painted, and soon, while it's in its prime. If Hepworth can't come, I'll get somebody else. I want that picture."

"And let's have some photographs of it. It's so perfect."

"All right, I'll take those myself,—to-morrow,—it's too late now."

"And me and Baby will sit in the middle of the composition! Won't that be touching!"

Patty laughed merrily, but Farnsworth said, "You bet you will! Be ready in the morning, for I'll want a lot of poses."

CHAPTER II

GUESTS ARRIVE

"I refuse to go a step further! This porch of wistaria is the most wonderful thing I ever saw in all my life! When I heard the name of the place, I thought it was crazy,—but of course I see now it's the only possible name! I don't care what's inside the house,—here I am,—and here I stay!"

Elise Farrington threw off her motor coat, and settling herself on the side seat of the porch, under the drooping bunches of purple bloom, looked quite as if she meant what she said.

Patty stepped out from the doorway and smiled at her visitor.

"All right, Elise," she said, "you may. I'll send out your dinner, and you can sleep here, too, if you like."

"No, I'll come in for my board and lodging, but all the rest of the time look for me here! I'm going to have some lavender frocks made,—dimities and organdies, and then I'll be part of the picture."

"Oh, do! I can't wear lavender or purple," Patty sighed.

"Nonsense! Of course you can. You only mean you've never tried. That bisque doll complexion of yours will stand any color. Let's both get wisteria-coloured frocks, and—"

Elise's plans were interrupted by the appearance of Farnsworth and two men who had arrived for the house party. These were our old friends, Philip Van Reypen and Chickering Channing.

Still a devoted admirer of pretty Patty, Van Reypen had become reconciled to his fate, and moreover had discovered his ability to take pleasure in the society of other charming young women.

Channing was the same old merry Chick, and he was exuberant in his praise of the beautiful home of the Farnsworths which he now saw for the first time.

"Great little old place!" he exclaimed, enthusiastically. "But why such an enormousness? Are you going to keep boarders?"

"Yes, if you'll stay," laughed Patty. "But, you see it was a bargain,—so we snapped it up."

"The old story," put in Bill. "Man built it,—went bankrupt, —had to sell at sacrifice. Along came we,—bought it,—every body happy!"

"I am," declared Elise; "this is the sort of place I've dreamed of. Beautiful nearby effects, and a long distance view beside. This porch for mine,—all the time I'm here."

"But you haven't seen the other places yet," Patty demurred. "There's a tea-porch—"

"Wistaria, too?"

"Yes, of course."

"Lead me to it!" and Elise jumped up, and made for the house.

Then they all strolled through the wide hall and out at the back door on to the tea-porch. This was furnished with white

Carolyn Wells

wicker tables and chairs, and indeed, was prepared for immediate use, for a maid was just bringing the cakes and crumpets as the party arrived.

"Goody!" cried Elise, "can we have tea now, Patty? I'm famished."

"Yes, indeed," and Patty took her place at the tea table with a matronly air, and began to pour for her guests.

"It's just as pretty as the other porch," Elise decided, looking critically at the festoons of wistaria, which was on three sides of the house. "But I'll adopt the first one. Anybody looking for me will find me there—'most always."

"We're always looking for you," said Channing, gallantly, as he took up his teacup, "and it is a comfort to know where to find you. Of late you've been inaccessible."

"Not to you," and Elise glanced coquettishly from under her eyelashes.

"To me, then," put in Van Reypen. "I've not seen you, Elise, since I came back from Over There. You've grown a lot, haven't you?"

"Taller?"

"Mercy no! I mean mentally. You seem more—more grown up like."

"Everybody is, since the war work. Yes, Phil, I have grown,—I hope."

"There, there," warned Patty; "no serious talk just now, please, —and no war talk. For the moment, I claim your attention to my new house and its surroundings."

"Some claim you've staked out," and Chick grinned. "I want

to see it all. And,—moreover,—I want to see the rest of the family!"

Patty beamed. "You dear!" she cried; "do you really want to see my daughter?"

"*My* daughter," Farnsworth added; "but I didn't know you chaps would be interested in our infant prodigy. I never cared about seeing other people's babies."

"I do," stoutly insisted Channing. "I'm a connoisseur on kiddies. Let me see him."

"He isn't him," laughed Patty, "he's a she."

"So much the better," Chick avowed. "I love girl babies. Where is she?"

"You can't see her now, she's probably asleep. To-morrow she'll be on exhibition. I hear a car! It must be Mona!"

"I'll go and fetch her," said Farnsworth, springing up, and after a short time he returned with two newcomers, Mona Farrington and her husband, Roger.

Then there was more greeting and exclamation and laughter, as the latest guests admired the new home, and accepted Patty in her becoming role of hostess.

"To think of little Patty as the chatelaine of this palatial menage!" said Roger, "and actually acting as if it belonged to her!"

"It isn't palatial," corrected Patty, "but it *does* belong to me, —that is, to me and my friend William. He vows I claim the baby for all my own property,—but I'll accord him a share in the place."

"It *all* belongs to me," said Farnsworth, with a careless sweep of a big arm. "The wistaria, Patty, the baby, and all!"

"That's right," agreed Roger, "keep up your air of authority as long as you can! I tried it,—but Mona soon usurped the position!"

"Nonsense!" and Mona smiled at her husband. "Don't you believe him, Patty. We go fifty-fifty on everything,—as to decisions, I mean. He gives in to my superior judgment half the time, and I let him have his own foolish way the other half. Follow my plan and you'll live happily, my dear."

"Are we your first company?" asked Elise.

"Yes,—except Father and Nan,—and a few calls from the neighbours. This is my first house-party. And I do want it to be a success, so I'm going to depend on you all to help me. If I do what I ought not to do,—or leave undone the things which I should ought to do,—check me up,—won't you, please?"

"We sure will," agreed Channing, "but something tells me you're going to prove an ideal hostess."

"She will," nodded Farnsworth, "she takes to hostessing like a duck to water. She even asked me what sort of smokes you chaps prefer."

"I hope you remembered," said Roger. "And when are they to be passed around?"

"Right now," said Patty, smiling and nodding to the maid who hovered near.

In truth, Patty was a born hostess, and without fuss or ostentation always had the comfort of her guests in mind. While not overburdened with a retinue of servants, she had enough to attend to everything she required of them; and her own knowledge and efficiency combined with her tact and real kindliness brought about a state of harmony in her household that might well have been envied by an older and more experienced matron.

Mrs. Chase, who had the nominal position of housekeeper, found herself strictly accountable to Patty for all she did, and as she was sensible enough to appreciate Patty's attitude, she successfully fulfilled the requirements of a butler or steward, and had general charge and oversight of all the housekeeping details.

"The way to keep house," said Patty to Mona and Elise, as she took them away with her, leaving the men to their "smokes," "is not so much to work yourself as to be able to make others work in the way you want them to."

"That's just it," agreed Mona, "and that's just what I can't do! Why, my servants rode over me so, and were so impudent and lazy, I just gave up housekeeping and went to a hotel to live. We had to,—there was no other way out."

"And how Roger hates it!" said Elise, who, as Roger's sister, thought herself privileged to comment.

A cloud passed over Mona's face. "He does," she admitted, "but what can I do? He hated worse the scenes we had when we were housekeeping."

"Perhaps conditions will get better now," said Patty, hopefully, "and you can try again, Mona, with better results."

"Maybe; and perhaps you can teach me. You used to teach me lots of things, Patty."

"All right,—I'll willingly do anything I can. Now, who wants to see my angel child? Or would you rather go to your rooms first?"

"No, indeed," cried Elise, "let me see her right now. If she's as pretty as the wistaria vine—oh, Patty, why don't you name her Wistaria?"

"Gracious, what a name! No, she's Fleurette,—or so Little Billee says. Anyway, here she is."

Patty led them to the nursery, and from the lacy draperies of the bassinette a smiling baby face looked up at them.

"What a heavenly kiddy!" Elise exclaimed, "Oh, Patty, what a daffodil head! Just a blur of yellow fuzz! And such blue eyes! She looks exactly like you! And exactly like Bill, too. Oh, I never saw such a darling baby. Let me take her,—mayn't I?"

"Yes, indeed. She's no glass-case baby."

Elise picked up the dear little bundle, and cooed and crooned in most approved fashion.

Apparently Fleurette understood, for she smiled and gurgled, and seemed to look upon Elise as an old friend.

Mona admired the baby but was more interested in the house.

"Show me everything," she begged Patty. "I want to see it all. Where's your linen closet?"

"My linen closet is a room," and Patty led them thither. "You see, we have such a lot of rooms and,—such a lot of linen, —that I took this little bedroom for a linen press. I had a carpenter put in the shelves and cupboards just as I wanted them,—and here's the result."

With justifiable pride, Patty showed her linen collection. Sheets, towels, tablecloths,—each sort in its place, each dozen held by blue ribbon bands, that fastened with little pearl buckles.

Other shelves held lace pieces, luncheon sets, boudoir pillow-cases, table scarfs, and all the exquisite embroidered bits that are the delight of the home lover.

"Perfectly wonderful!" Elise declared; "looks just like a shop in Venice or Nice. How do you keep them so tidy? and where did you ever get so many?"

"Oh, I've done quite some shopping to get our Lares and Penates together, and Bill let me get whatever I wanted in the house furnishing line. Yes, this linen room is my joy and my pride. See, *this* cupboard is all curtains. I do love to have fresh curtains as often as I want them."

"Well, it's all like Fairyland," Mona said. "I have beautiful things, too, but they don't look like this. They're all in a jumble on the shelves, and everything is hodge-podge."

"Oh, well, you're just as happy," laughed Patty. "I chance to be naturally tidy, and I just love to potter over my things, and keep them in place. Some time I'll show you Baby's wardrobe. Her little things are too dear for anything. But now I'll take you to your rooms. This is yours, Elise. I picked out this one for you, because it's lavender,—and I know that's your favorite colour."

"And the wistaria vine is looking in at the windows!" Elise noted, with joy. "Oh, Patty, I won't live on the porch, either, I'll live up here."

It *was* a beautiful room. A deep seated bay-window, with latticed panes, opened into a profusion of wistaria blooms, and the fragrance filled the whole place. The furniture was of ivory enamel and the appointments were of various harmonious shades of lavender. A *chaise-longue* was well supplied with lace pillows and a nearby stand and reading-lamp hinted at the comfortable enjoyment of a tempting array of new books.

Pansies and violets were in small bowls, and on a table stood an enormous vase full of trailing branches of wistaria.

Carolyn Wells

"What a picture!" and Elise stood in the middle of the floor, looking about her. "Patty, you're a wonder! I don't care if you have shoals of servants, you fixed up this room,—I know you did."

"Of course I did,—with Mrs. Chase to help me. She's a treasure,—she catches on to my ways so quickly. Glad you like it, Elise, honey. Now settle yourself here,—your bags will be up in a minute,—and I'll put Mona in her niche."

"I'm coming too," and Elise went with the others to the rooms designed for Mona and Roger.

"This is my Royal Suite," laughed Patty, as she ushered them into a charming apartment done up in handsome English chintz.

"It suits me," and Mona nodded approval. "You had this done by a professional, Patty."

"It was here when we bought the house. You see, some rooms were already furnished, when the man decided to sell it. And of these, such as we liked we kept as they were. This is especially fine chintz and also good workmanship, so as it is so imposing in effect, we call it the Royal Suite. Father and Nan adored it, and you and Roger are the next Royal guests."

"It's great," said Elise, "not half as pretty as mine, but more dignified and gorgeous."

The chintz was patterned with tropical birds and foliage and as the hangings were many and elaborate the effect *was* gorgeous. The bathroom was spacious and fully equipped, and as Mona's things had arrived she turned to instruct the maid who was already unpacking them.

"Come back with me to my room," said Elise, as she and Patty went down the hall.

"Just for a minute, then, for I must go and sort out the rest of my visitors. I am putting Philip and Chick over in the west wing, far removed from the nursery, for I don't want them imagining they are kept awake by the night thoughts of my child. And, I must confess, Fleurette has a way of tuning up in the wee, small hours! However, we had the nursery walls muffled, so I don't think you'll be disturbed. Isn't this outlook fine, Elise?"

"Beautiful," and Elise joined Patty at the bay-window. "This is the most effective room I ever saw, and so comfy."

"And here's your bath," Patty opened the door to a bathroom of white-tiled and silver daintiness. "Now you've time for a tub and a rest before dinner. So I'm going to leave you. Come down at eight,—or sooner, if you like."

Housewifely Patty ran away, happy in her new role of hostess to a house party.

The men still sat on the tea-porch, smoking, and talking over the political situation.

"Here you are again," Chick greeted her; "but where's the child? I must see that youngster to-night. I've—I've brought her a present."

"Oh, well, come along, then," said Patty; "if you're really so anxious to meet the young lady,—why wait?"

The two went up to the nursery, and though a little surprised at the unexpected call, Nurse Winnie made no objection.

"Here's your new friend," and Patty lifted Fleurette out of her pillows and presented her to Chick.

"What a beauty!" he cried, as he saw the golden curls and the big blue eyes. "And so intelligent!"

"Of course! Did you think she'd look vacant?"

"They often do," said Chick, sagely. "Why, my cousin's baby looks positively idiotic at times,—but this mite,—she knows it all!"

And Fleurette did look wise. Being in benign mood, she smiled at the big man who held her so gently, and put out a tentative fist toward his face.

"Born flirt," he declared, "just like her mother! Well, Patty, she's a wonder-child,—oh, I know 'em!—and I hereby constitute myself her godfather, without waiting to be asked."

"Good! We accept the honour. Make a bow, Fleurette."

"No, the honour is mine. She doesn't quite take it all in, yet,—but in days to come, she may feel real need of a godfather and I'll be there!"

"What do godfathers do? I never had any."

"I'm not quite sure, myself. I'm going to get a field-book,—or First Lessons in Godfathering, or something like that. But, anyway, I'm hers! Oh, Patty, she's going to grow up a beauty! Did you ever see such eyes!"

Patty laughed at Chick's enthusiasm, which was too patently genuine to be mere polite flattery, and entirely agreed in his opinion as to the good looks of the small Fleurette.

"What did you bring her?" she asked, and Chick drew from his pocket a set of small gold pins.

"For her bibs and tuckers," he explained. "At least that's what they told me at the shop. I don't know much about such things."

"They're just right," Patty said, "and they're her very first present,—outside the family. Thank you a thousand times, —you're very thoughtful, Chick."

"I hoped you'd like 'em," and the big, warm-hearted chap smiled with gratification. "Dress her up in them to-morrow, will you?"

And Patty promised she would.

CHAPTER III

BETTY GALE

Seated at the head of her own dinner table that evening, Patty felt decidedly in her element. Always of a hospitable nature, always efficient in household matters, she played her role of hostess with a sweet simplicity and a winning grace that charmed all her guests.

Farnsworth, opposite her at the big, round table, was a quiet, dignified and well-mannered host. He had not Patty's native ability to entertain, but he was honestly anxious that his guests should be pleased and he did all in his power to help along. Patty had coached him on many minor points, for Little Billee had been brought up in simple surroundings and unaccustomed to what he at first called Patty's frills and fal-lals.

But she had convinced him that dainty laces and shining silver were to be used for his daily fare and not merely as "company fixings," and being adaptable, the good-natured man obediently fell in with her wishes.

And now he was as deft and handy with his table appointments as Patty herself, and quite free from self-consciousness or awkwardness.

"You've made me all over, Patty," he would sometimes say; "now, I really like these dinky doo-daddles better than the 'old oaken bucket' effects on which I was brought up!"

And then Patty would beg him to tell her more about his early days and his wild Western life in the years before she knew him.

It was her great regret that Bill had no parents, nor indeed any near relatives. An only child, and early orphaned, he had lived a few years with a cousin and then had shifted for himself. A self-made man,—as they are styled,—he had developed fine business ability, and had also managed to acquire a familiarity with the best in literature. Patty was continually astonished by his ready references and his quotations from the works of the best authors.

Indeed, the room he took the deepest interest in furnishing in their new home was the library.

For the purpose he selected the largest room in the house. It had been designed as a drawing-room or ballroom; but Farnsworth said that its location and outlook made it an ideal library. He had an enormous window cut, that filled almost the whole of one side of the room, and which looked out upon a beautiful view, especially at sunset.

Then the furnishings were chosen for comfort and ease as well as preserving the dignified effect that should belong to a library. The book cases were filled with the books already owned by the two and new ones were chosen and bought by degrees as they were desired or needed.

The reference portion was complete and the cases devoted to poetry and essays well filled. Fiction, too, of the lasting kind, and delightful books of travel, biography and humour.

There were reading chairs, arranged near windows and with handy tables; there were desks, perfectly appointed; racks of new books and magazines; portfolios of pictures, and cosy window seats and *tete-a-tetes*.

There were a few fine pictures, and many little intimate

sketches by worth-while pencils or brushes. And there were treasured books, valuable intrinsically or because of their inscriptions, that Farnsworth had collected here and there.

Small wonder, then, that the library was the favourite room in the house and that after dinner Patty proposed they go there for their coffee.

"Some room!" ejaculated Chick Channing, as they sauntered in and stood about, gazing at the wealth of books.

"Glorious!" agreed Mona, who had a mere pretence of a library in her own home. "I didn't know you were so literary, Patty."

"Oh, I'm not. It's Little Billee's gigantic intellect that planned this room, and he's the power that keeps it going. Every week he sends up a cartload of new books—"

"Oh, come, now, Patty,—I haven't bought a book for a fortnight!" laughed Farnsworth. "But I've just heard of a fine old edition of Ike Walton that I can get at—"

"There, there, my son, don't get started on your hobby," implored Channing. "We're ignoramuses, Mona and I, and we want to talk about less highbrow subjects."

"Count me on your side," said a smiling girl, whose big gray eyes took on a look of awe at the turn the conversation had taken. "I don't know if Ike Walton is a book or a steamboat!"

The speaker was Beatrice Gale, a neighbour of the Farnsworths. She was pretty and saucy looking,—a graceful sprite, with a dimpled chin, and soft brown hair, worn in moppy bunches over her ears. She was called Betty by her friends, and Patty and Bill had already acquired that privilege.

"Now, Betty," and Patty shook her head at her, "you are a college graduate as well as a debutante,—you *must* know old Ike!"

"But I don't! You see, my debut meant so much more to me than my commencement, that all I ever learned at college flew out of my head to make room for all I'm going to learn in society."

"Have you much left to learn?" asked Elise, looking at the piquant face that seemed to show its owner decidedly conversant with the ways of the world,—at least, her own part in it.

"Oh, indeed, yes! I only know how to smile and dance. I'm going to learn flirting, coquetry and getting engaged!"

"You're ambitious, little one," remarked Van Reypen. "Have you chosen your instructors?"

"I'm sure you won't need any," put in Elise, who was already jealous of Philip's interested looks at the new girl. "I think you could pass an efficiency examination already!"

"You ought to know," said Betty, with such an innocent and demure look at Elise, that it was difficult to determine whether she meant to be impertinent or not.

"Let me conduct the examination," said Philip; "shall it be public,—or will you go with me into a—a classroom?" and he looked toward the small "den" that opened from the library.

"Oh, have it public!" exclaimed Mona. "Let us all hear it"

"All right," and pretty Betty smiled, non-chalantly. "Go ahead, Professor."

"I will. You know these examinations begin by matching words. I say one word, and you say whatever word pops into your head first."

"That's easy enough. Proceed."

"Arden."

"Forest. I always thought this place ought to have been named the Forest of Arden, because—"

"Don't talk so much. You must say one word only. Concentrate."

"Silence."

"Oh, concentrate wasn't the *word*! I said that to you—"

"I thought you were talking to me *all* the time!"

"I am. Now be still! Horse."

"How can I pass my examination if I'm to be still? Wagon."

"Aeroplane."

"You."

"How did you know that I was an aviator?"

"Never mind; go on with the game."

"All right. Beaux."

"Flattery."

"Chaperon."

"Hoodwink."

"Oh, you rascal! Mother."

"Father."

"Father."

"Money."

"Soft-boiled egg."

"Messy."

"American Beauties."

"Mr. Grant,—he often sends them to me."

"Music."

"Dancing."

"You pass. Now for to see if you're thoroughly grounded in the common branches. Grammar, first. What's a noun, and give examples."

"A noun's a name. As, candy, heart, slipper."

"What's a compound noun?"

"Two names,—as chicken salad,—Philip Van Reypen,—moonlight."

"What's a mood?"

"Something you fall into,—as a ditch,—or love."

"What is an article?"

"A piece of fancy work for sale at a fair."

"What's a conjunction?"

"Anything that joins,—as the marriage ceremony, or hooks and eyes."

"Good. Now for arithmetic. If you are at home of an evening, and a chap calls on you, and then I come to call, and take half your attention from him, what is left?"

"The chap!"

"Right! Now, definitions. What do you mean by forever?"

"Until to-morrow!" returned Betty, laughing.

"Never?"

"Not until to-morrow!"

"How do you spell No?"

"Y-e-s."

"Oh, Betty," exclaimed Patty, laughing, "I didn't know you were so witty!"

"Good gracious! don't call me *that!* Here, stop this examination right now! I *won't* be called witty. Why, don't you know—

    "'Though you're sweet and though you're pretty,
    Men won't love you if you're witty!'

"I'm *always* afraid of not being loved!"

Miss Gale looked so frightened at this very idea, that they all broke into laughter.

"You should worry!" declared Bill. "You haven't enough wit to do any great harm. Or, at least, if you have, you've compensating foolishness—I mean—that is—"

"There, there, Billee," counselled Patty, "you'd better stop,— you're just getting in deeper with every word."

"Oh, it's all right," and Beatrice shrugged her shoulders, "I need to be brought up with a round turn now and then. I'm too intellectual,—I know."

She purposely assumed a vacant, stupid expression and folded her hands helplessly in her lap.

"She's a hummer," Channing remarked in an aside to Patty, as further hilarity followed Betty's fooling.

"I like her lots," Patty returned. "She's a frivolous little thing, but thoroughly sweet and dear. She adores Fleurette."

"Aha, little mother! So that's the way to your good graces, is it? I too adore Fleurette."

"But you're already in my good graces,—and have been for years."

"So? Then,"—Chick's tone grew wheedlesome,—"invite me up here often,—won't you?"

"Now I *should* have thought you meant because of my daughter's charms, if your glance hadn't wandered toward Miss Gale, even as you spoke!"

"Both, fair lady,—both. I adore Fleurette as the delightful daughter of a delightful mother. May I not also admire the delightful neighbour?"

"Indeed, you may. And you have a standing invitation to come up here as often as you like. I'm going to entertain a lot this spring and summer,—and you're a really useful house guest"

"Thanks, indeed! How do I qualify?"

"By your nice, kind, entertaining qualities. You're an all-round nice man, Chick,—and I don't care who knows my opinion. And now, do you go and make up to Elise."

"Yes, ma'am. Between you and me, ma'am,—she's a bit miffed—not?"

"Hush! Run along and make yourself so agreeable that she'll forget everybody else."

Of a truth Elise was a little disturbed. For she was of a jealous and self-seeking disposition, and resented any attentions that were not given to her. The advent of this bright and sparkling young girl,—probably three or four years younger than herself, made her suddenly feel neglected, and it displeased her.

Mona noticed it, and smiled to herself. But Patty truly regretted it, for she had taken a decided fancy to Beatrice Gale, and as they were neighbours, she knew the girl would be often at Wistaria Porch. And as she had planned to have Elise with her often, also, she saw breakers ahead, unless the two could be reconciled.

Patty was a born peacemaker, but she also knew that a jealous nature is not easily placated. And she foresaw that Philip Van Reypen would be the "bone of contention."

After Patty's marriage, Philip, a disappointed suitor, had declared himself a confirmed bachelor. And though Elise would have looked with satisfaction on his change of heart, it had not yet occurred.

Patty had hoped,—and thought,—that Philip would marry her cousin, Helen Barlow; but neither of the parties had seen it in that light, and Helen had since married her long persistent wooer, Chester Wilde.

This left Van Reypen entirely unattached, and Elise,—it could be seen by any onlooker,—was not at all averse to his company.

And Van Reypen liked her, for Elise was pretty and charming. But when things didn't go as she wished them to, she had a habit of sulking which was far from attractive.

So, the very apparent interest that Philip showed in this new chit of a girl,—as Elise dubbed Betty to herself,—was as iron entering her soul.

However, she was clever enough to hide her real feelings, and she welcomed Chick Channing with a cordial smile.

"Let's go for a stroll round the verandahs," he proposed, and Elise consented.

"Want a wrap? though it's warm for April," he said, as they went out the door.

"No, thank you, I love the fresh air," and Elise waved her white arm upward, and entwined it in the wistaria blossoms. "I've adopted this porch,—I shall probably be with Patty a lot this summer. You'll come up—now and then?"

"Oh, yes; it's the most charming house to visit, don't you think?"

"Great! Patty is an ideal hostess, and Bill's a dear!"

"And the kiddy,—don't leave her out"

"Oh, she's an angel. But a bit unfledged, as yet."

"Of course. But such a darling! By the way, I'm her godfather."

"Oh, are you? Then I'll be her godmother! She ought to have both."

"Certainly. Though I think I heard that Miss Gale has the position."

"Of course she has! That girl appropriates everything! I think she's too fresh!"

"You mean that for a compliment, I'm sure. Yes, she is,—she's like a dewy daisy—"

"Dewy daisy, nothing! She isn't so childlike as she wants to appear!"

"There now, Elise, don't talk like that! It doesn't sound pretty,—and goodness knows *you've* no reason to be jealous."

"What?" asked Elise, already mollified.

"Why, you, with your established place in this household, and in our set,—mustn't stoop to be—jealous—of a little schoolgirl!"

"Oh, I'm *not*! How dare you hint it?"

"Then don't act so. Take my advice, Lisa, and don't show even the appearance of that sort of thing. It reacts,—you know."

Elise did know,—she knew Chick was telling her the truth, and telling it, too, only in the kindest spirit of real friendship.

She bit her lip in annoyance, and said, sharply, "Don't abuse the privilege of an old friend, Chick."

"I don't mean to,—honest I don't, Elise. Forgive me if I've offended you."

"Oh, you haven't. That's all right. Have you ever met this Gale girl before?"

"No; but she sat next me at dinner, and she told me about herself. It seems she has a wonderful brother—"

"She has!" It was amazing how Elise brightened up. "Why wasn't he invited this evening?"

"He's away from home just now,—will return next week,—I

think she said. Get on your warpaint and feathers! See, the conquering heroine comes!"

"Stop teasing, Chick. I do like to meet strangers, and if Patty's neighbour is attractive—"

"Patty's neighbour's brother,—you mean?"

"I do! If he's attractive, it'll add to my pleasure when visiting Patty,—won't it?"

"It sure will,—and, may I say it? You'll add to his pleasure, I've no doubt."

"Very pretty, Chick. You *are* a nice boy."

"Thank you, ma'am. But I won't be in it, when the brother appears on the scene, I fear! So, to make hay while the sun shines, won't you go in and dance with me? I hear the light fantastics tripping in the hall."

They went in and found all of the party keeping time to the gay music of the big victrola, and they joined the swaying couples.

As they passed Betty Gale and Van Reypen, Elise overheard her saying, "You're awfully good to me,—and you've only just met me to-night!"

Phil's reply was lost as they danced away, but Elise realised that it was an eager expression of his desire that they should meet again, and soon, and her demon of jealousy once more up-reared his ugly head.

But she concealed it,—outwardly, at least,—and when the time came, she was so cordial and sweet to Miss Gale that a friendship pact was sealed between them.

CHAPTER IV

A NEW RELATIVE

May came in with the sunshine and balmy days that are popularly supposed to belong to that month, but which do not always materialise.

Wistaria Porch was fairly basking in the sunshine, and the flower gardens were already showing their early blooms. The tulip beds were a blaze of bright glory and hyacinths and daffodils added their sweetness and beauty.

"Such a heavenly place!" Patty exclaimed as she and Little Billee strolled along the garden paths in the late afternoon. "I'm glad we have this week-end to ourselves,—I love to have guests, but once in a while,—you know—"

"I do know!" declared Farnsworth, "and I'd be willing to have 'em twice in a while—"

"Have what?"

"Week-ends alone with you! Oh, I like company, too,—have all you want, but now and then—just now and then, a family party looks good to me! Where's our blessed child at the moment?"

"She ought to be here,—it's time. Winnie usually brings her for her afternoon visit to her proud parents. And here she comes! Here's mudder's own Poggly-woggly Pom-pom head!"

"What delightful names you invent! Let me have a try at it! Here's Fodder's own Piggly-winktum! There, how's that?"

"Perfectly horrid! Sounds like a pig!"

"All right, let's try again. Who's the airiest, fairiest, tiny mite? Who's the pinky-goldiest Smiley-eyes in the whole world? Here she is!" and big Bill took the baby, from nurse's arms, and flung her high in the air, catching her deftly on her descent, while Patty held her breath in apprehension. She knew perfectly well Bill wouldn't let the child fall,—and yet, accidents had occurred,—and the crowing baby might squirm out of the watchful father's arms.

But no accident happened and the two had their usual afternoon romp.

Little Fleurette knew her father and adored the big, comfortable man who held her so firmly and tossed her up so delightfully.

"Now, it's my turn,—give her to me," said Patty, at last. Then Bill deposited the child in her mother's arms, and the little one nestled there contentedly. She was a good baby, and rarely cried or fretted. Healthy and strong, she bade fair to become a fine big woman some day, and Patty's leaping mind had already planned out her whole lifetime!

"I think I'll send her to the Mortimer School," she said, musingly.

"Why, that's a finishing school!" exclaimed Bill, knowing of the fashionable establishment.

"Yes; I mean when she's ready to be 'finished,'" said Patty, calmly. "Before that, she'll go to Kindergarten,—and some other school, I suppose."

"I suppose she will; but we'll have a few years of her company here, at home, won't we, before her schooldays begin?"

"Yes, of course, we're having them now. But they go so fast! Oh, Little Billee, *all* the days fly so fast,—I can't realise we've been married nearly two years—"

"Nonsense! A year and nearly two months—"

"Well, it soon *will* be two years! I never saw the time fly so! It goes like a Bandersnatch!"

"Does that mean you're so happy, Patty?"

"It means exactly that! Oh, I want to live forever! I am so happy! I didn't know life with you and Fleurette would be so beautiful as it is!"

"Is it, dearest? I'm so glad," and the big man looked at his dainty, sweet little wife with his whole soul in his fine clear blue eyes.

"Your eyes are wonderful, Billee, dear," said Patty, meeting his glance lovingly; "did your mother have blue eyes,—or your father?"

"Both of them did. I was thought to look more like mother, as a kiddy,—but they were both fair haired and blue eyed."

"You never knew your mother much, did you?"

"No, she died when I was very small. And father, when I was about ten. Then, as I've told you, I lived four years with Aunt Amanda—"

"In Arizona?"

"Yes; in a small settlement,—hardly even a village,—called Horner's Corners."

Patty laughed. "What a darling name! How could anybody call a place that! Suppose it had grown to be a large city."

"Then they would probably have changed the name. Perhaps they have already done so,—I haven't heard from there for years."

"Why didn't you keep up your relatives' acquaintance?"

"Well, Aunt Amanda died, later, and her husband never cared much for me, anyhow. So we drifted apart, and never drifted together again."

"Wasn't your aunt your mother's sister?"

"Oh, Lord, no! She was not really my aunt, at all. She was a cousin of my father's and when she took me in, I called her auntie. But they only took me because they wanted my help on the place, and I worked hard for them four years. They gave me no affection, nor even thanks for my services, and as I couldn't learn anything or make any sort of progress in that God-forsaken valley, I left them and shifted for myself."

"And made a great success of the shifting!" Patty's eyes glowed as she looked at her big handsome husband.

"Yes, I found you! And, incidentally that little flower of loveliness that's going to sleep against your breast."

"So she is! Pretty thing!" Patty gazed adoringly at the baby and then handed her over to the nurse, who returned for her charge.

"Tell me more about Horner's Corners," Patty resumed, as they remained seated on the porch, after Fleurette's departure.

"Not much to tell. It consisted of a store and post-office,—a church and school,—and forty or fifty small houses. Uncle Thorpe's place was a mile out from the Corners, proper, and I used to trudge back and forth every day for the mail, and for provisions. And part of the time I went to school. The teacher was a nice young girl, but we boys led her a dance! How we *did* plague her!" and Bill laughed at the recollection.

"Any children in your aunt's family?"

"One; a little baby girl, named Azalea."

"What a pretty name! Where is she now?"

"I don't know. Right there, probably. Let me see. I was ten when I went there. But she wasn't born then. When I left, that child was about a year old, I guess. She must be about seventeen or so, now."

"And she's your only living relative?"

"The only one I know anything about. Mother's people were English,—none of them over here. No near relatives, anyhow, for she was an only child. Dad was, too, for that matter. Little Zaly,—that's what they called her, is about the last leaf on the tree."

"Let's ask her to visit us, can't we? I do want to know your people; and if she's all the people there are, I want to know her."

"Why, child, I don't know anything about her,—I don't even know if she's still in the land of the living."

"Can't you write and find out?"

"Why, I suppose so. But *why* do you want her? She's probably an awkward, countrified little thing—"

"I don't care for that! She's your kin, and I'm prepared to love her for that reason."

"That's a dear thing for you to say, Patty mine, but you may get more than you bargain for. Suppose you invite Azalea and Uncle Thorpe himself comes trotting along, too!"

"Well, I could even live through that! I don't suppose he'd bite me!"

"But I'm quite sure he wouldn't fit into your scheme of things entire! Oh, let sleeping dogs lie, Pattibelle. Take me for my whole family,—I'm a host in myself."

"You are,—my lord and master,—you sure are! But, all the same, I must hunt up your little cousin. Of course her father can't come, if he isn't invited. And I'd like to know the child. I might do something for her,—be of some real help to her, I mean. Maybe she's longing to get East and have the advantages I could give her."

"Maybe she's longing to stay put in her native desert."

"In that case, she can say so. I shan't compel her to come! Let me write her, anyway, mayn't I, Little Billee?"

"Of course you may. You may write to anybody you wish; to the Sultan of Kasharabad, if you like."

"Is he your relative?"

"He may be,—for all I know. Some family trees branch widely."

"Well, give me Azalea's address,—I'm going to open a correspondence, at least."

"No address, that I know of, except Miss Azalea Thorpe, Horner's Corners, Arizona."

"I'll write, if only for the fun of addressing a letter there. I never heard such a funny name for a place!"

Patty tore up two or three letters before she finally composed one that suited her. It was not easy to know what attitude to take toward such a complete stranger, and with no knowledge of what sort of a girl she was writing to. But she at last sent off this:

MY DEAR AZALEA:

I am the wife of your cousin, William Farnsworth. Though you do not remember him, your father will tell you about him. At any rate, as you are of his kin, I want you to come and make us a visit—that is, if you care to. We have a lovely home, not far from New York City, and I would do my best to make you happy and give you a good time. You may not want to come,—indeed, you may have moved away from your native town, and may never even get this letter. But if you do get it, write me, at any rate, and tell me what you think about a trip East. We both send love and hope to hear from you soon.

Affectionately yours,

PATTY FARNSWORTH.

"You see," Patty explained to Bill, as she read the letter to him, "it may be she can't afford such a trip. But I didn't like to hint at that, so I asked her to write me what she thinks about it. If she thinks she can't spend so much money, then we can offer to get her ticket."

"Very thoughtful and very delicately done, my dearest. You have the kindest heart a little blue-eyed girl ever possessed."

"Not entirely disinterested, though. I do want to have some of your people under our roof,—and this is my first attempt. If it fails, I shall look up some of your English relatives."

"Yes, we will do that some day. I'd like to round them up

myself. Mother's tales of her childhood home,—as retold me by my father,—sounded delightful. They had old country estates, and—"

"And ancestral halls! Hung with old armour! Oh, Little Billee, what fun to take Fleurette there! Portraits of her ancestors smiling down at her from the oaken walls of the long picture gallery—"

"Patty, Patty! how you *do* run on! I don't know that there are any picture galleries at all."

"Oh, of course there are. They're bound to be there. And maybe a family ghost! A spectre, that stalks the corridors when one of the family is about to die—"

"Hush! You bad child! What awful ideas!"

"I've just been reading a story about a family spectre. I think they're *most* interesting."

"Well, we'll cut out the spook show. *I've* no liking for clanking chains and hollow groans!"

*　*　*　*　*

Impatiently Patty waited for the answer to her letter, and one day it came.

Farnsworth was in New York on business, and so she put it away unopened until his return.

"Goody girl!" he cried, when she told him. "Nice of you, dear, to let us have the first reading together."

"Oh, I couldn't gobble it up alone,—I like everything better if I have it with you."

And so they sat side by side on the porch, and read the long looked for missive.

*   *   *   *   *

"DEAR COUSIN PATTY;" it began.

I was so surprised and pleased to get your letter I hardly knew
what to do. It seemed as if the dream of my life had at last
come true. I've always wanted to go East,—to see New
York,—oh, I'm so excited I can hardly write! And dear Cousin
William! How kind of him to tell you about me,—for I was a
very small baby when he was here. My father has told me all
about it. When shall I start? I accept your invitation with joy. I
have saved up my money and I have enough, I think, for the
ticket. How much does it cost? But I can find out somehow.
Father sends his respects and he says I may go. I am all ready.
Can't you telegraph me, so I can go soon?

With grateful thanks,
I am yours very sincerely,
AZALEA THORPE.

"Well," said Bill, "what do you think of that for a letter?"

He looked thoughtfully at Patty, as he spoke.

"Why," she hesitated,—"I think it's a very nice letter—"

"Wait, now,—be honest!"

"Well, I—oh, I don't know,—but I looked for a little more—
simplicity, I guess. This sounds as if she had resorted to a
'Complete Letter-Writer' for help."

"Just what I thought, exactly! But I don't know as we can
blame her if she did. The poor child is doubtless unversed in
polite correspondence, and she did her best,—but she felt she
needed a little more elegance of construction and so forth, and
she picked out some dressy phrases from the book."

"It doesn't matter, anyway," said Patty, generously, "she's glad to come, and so I'm glad to have her. Let's telegraph at once,—shall us?"

"Yes; but I don't like that haste of hers. It strikes me queer."

"Queer, how? She's impatient to start,—that's all. What else could it mean?"

"I don't know, I'm sure. But the whole letter's queer,—if you ask me!"

"I *do* ask you,—and I ask you *how* it's queer."

"It's so,—so jumbly,—incoherent,—choppy."

"Pooh! don't criticise the lack of style in that poor country child. I'll teach her to write letters,—and I won't let her know I'm teaching her, either."

"You'll teach her lots of things,—I know,—and in that dear, gentle way of yours, that couldn't hurt or offend anybody. Well, I'll telegraph, then, for her to come ahead. What else shall I say?"

"Tell her what road to take, and all directions you can think of. Though it sounds to me, as if she thought she would have no difficulty as to travel."

"Sounds that way to me, too; but I suppose her father can look after such details. Queer message from her father."

"Not at all. You said he wasn't overfond of you, so as he sends his respects to you, I don't think you need ask for more."

"If she does start right off,—and I'm pretty sure she will, —she'll be here in a week or so."

"Of course; but I'll be ready for her. I'll give her the yellow

Carolyn Wells

room. It's big and sunny and has a lovely bath and dressing-room. It's all in order, too, I'll just make some soft lacy pillows and give it some little personal touches and it will be all ready for her. Oh, Billee,—think what a lot we can do for her!"

Patty's eyes glowed with the anticipation of aiding the little country girl, but Farnsworth was not so sanguine.

"You're running a risk, girlie," he said. "Suppose she turns out impossible. The fact of her being my relative doesn't quite canonise her, you know. Perhaps she *isn't* a saint."

"Now, now, old calamity howler,—I don't want her to be a saint! I hope and expect she'll be a sweet, docile nature, and her lack of culture, if any, I shall try to remedy. Her lack of familiarity with social customs and all that, I *know* I can remedy. Oh, I expect a busy time with her,—and I know I shall have to be tactful and kind,—but don't you think I can be?"

Farnsworth kissed the wistful, questioning face upturned to his and assured her that she most certainly could!

So Patty gaily set about her preparations of the pretty guest chamber. She hoped Azalea liked yellow,—most girls did,—but if not, she could easily be moved to the pink guest room.

This yellow room, however, was so well adapted for a young girl. There was a long French window that opened on the dearest little balcony, where the wistaria clambered and made a delightful shade. There was an alcove, where stood a Chippendale writing desk, and a revolving book rack. There was a sewing corner, with a fully furnished work-stand; and there was a soft puffy couch, with a pile of down pillows and a fluffy yellow afghan. And yet there was ample room for the bed, with its dimity draperies, and the fascinating toilet table, with its bewildering array of ivory fittings.

Uncertain of her guest's tastes, Patty put out few books, only a story or two of general interest and a couple of new magazines. All such matters could be attended to after she had sized up the newcomer.

On the day she was expected, Patty arranged the flowers in the yellow room herself.

Naturally, she chose azaleas, and some of a lovely soft tint of buff harmonised with pale pink ones. White ones too, with a bit of green foliage, until the room was a bower of beauty. Not overdone, though. Patty never made the mistake of too many flowers,—fond as she was of them.

A last affectionate survey of the room convinced her that all was exactly as it should be, and with a happy little sigh of contentment she went down to the porch to await the arrival of the guest, for Farnsworth had gone to the station to meet her, and they were due now at any minute.

CHAPTER V

THAT AWFUL AZALEA

The car came along the driveway and stopped in front of the porch where Patty sat.

Farnsworth stepped out, with a cheery "Here we are!" and Patty rose to greet the visitor.

Up the steps toward her flew a figure which, as Patty afterward described it, seemed like a wild Indian! A slight, wiry figure, rather tall and very awkward, and possessed of a nervous force that expressed itself in muscular activity.

"Oh, how do you do?" the girl cried, explosively. "You're Cousin Patty,—aren't you?" But even as she spoke, she stumbled on the steps, pitched forward, falling on Patty, and but for Farnsworth's quick action would have knocked her down.

"Jiminy crickets! Ain't I the tangle-foot! Guess I'm getting in bad at the very start. Hope I didn't hurt you."

"Not at all," said Patty, recovering her poise, both mental and physical. "You are very welcome, Azalea. Will you sit here a few minutes before we go in the house?"

"Sure! I'll spill myself right into this double-decker!"

She threw herself into a long wicker lounging-seat, of the steamer-chair type, and stretched out her feet in evident enjoyment of the relaxation.

"Well, this is comfort, after travelling cross country for days and days! I say, Cousin, it was awful good of you to ask me."

"Think so?" and Patty tried to smile pleasantly. She avoided catching Bill's eye, for the poor man was overcome with shame and consternation that his relative should be so impossible.

"Yep,—I do. My! this place of yours is swell. I never saw such a grand house—close to. You're rich, ain't you, Cousin William?"

"So, so," Farnsworth replied, gazing at the girl in a sort of horrified fascination. "You've changed since last we met," he went on, in an endeavour to make casual conversation.

"Well, yes, I s'pose so. They tell me I was a squalling young one when you were at the Corners. Was I a terror?"

"Not then!" Bill wanted to answer, but of course he didn't.

"Not at all," he said, pleasantly. "You were a pretty baby—"

"But greatly changed,—hey?"

The girl gave him a quick glance. She was not ill-looking, as to features and colouring, but her whole effect was unattractive,—even repelling.

She had flashing black eyes, which darted from one object to another in a jerky, inquisitive way. Her scarlet lips parted over white, even teeth, but her lower lip hung, and her half-open mouth gave her an air of ignorance, often accompanied by rude staring.

Her black hair was concealed by a coarse straw hat, untrimmed save for some gaudy flowers embroidered on the straw with crude coloured wools.

"How do you like my hat?" Azalea asked suddenly. "Just the shape of a horse's hat, isn't it? But it's all the go. This dress is, too,—hope you like it,—I do."

The dress in question was a "sport suit" of a large-sized green and black check. It was cheap material, and badly cut, and its ill-fitting coat hung on Azalea's slim shoulders in baggy wrinkles. Her blouse was bright pink Georgette, beaded with scarlet beads, and altogether, perhaps her costume could not have been worse chosen or made up,—at least, from Patty's point of view.

She ignored the question about the hat, and asked the girl as to her journey.

"O.K.," Azalea returned. "Had a bang-up time. Made friends all along the line. Some of 'em coming to see me. Hope you'll like 'em."

She stretched out luxuriously in the long chair, throwing her arms above her head, and crossing her feet, which were dressed with "gun metal" stockings and shoes. Her hat was pushed awry, and wisps of hair fell at either side of her face.

"Now, perhaps you'd like to go to your room," suggested Patty, at her wits' end what to do with such an unconventional person.

"Nixy; I'm too comfortable here! I'll chuck my hat, and just enjoy myself."

Off came the hat, and was pitched on the floor. Azalea ran her fingers through her hair, making it a little more disordered than before. It was pretty hair,—or, rather would have been, if it were better cared for. Dark, almost black, with a slight inclination to curl, it was bunched into a tousled knot that was far from picturesque.

"Oh, come," said Patty, jumping up, for she couldn't stand the girl's uncouth actions another minute. "Come along with me, Azalea. You must dress for dinner soon,—and some one might come to call now. We'll have tea in your room, if you like."

"Tea! I never drink it. I like coffee,—for breakfast,—or cocoa. But see here, Cousin, don't you make any difference for me. I ain't company, you know,—just let me be one of the family, won't you?"

Many retorts flashed through Patty's mind, but she only said, "Certainly, Azalea. We want you to be one of us."

Farnsworth was silent. The man was really aghast. What had he brought on poor little Patty! He didn't excuse himself with the thought that it was Patty's doing, not his, that Azalea was there at all, but he felt personally to blame for having such a relative and for having her there in their home. He looked helplessly at Patty, with such despair in his kind eyes, that she ran over and kissed him, in spite of the fact that they were not alone.

Azalea giggled. "That's right," she said, affably; "don't mind me! Just go right on spoonin' even when I'm around. I don't mind. And I don't wonder you took to her, Cousin William. She's a peach, for fair,—ain't she?"

"She certainly is," said Farnsworth, forcing a polite smile, but conscious of a strong desire to choke his new-found relative.

His utterly discouraged face roused Patty to fresh efforts at hospitality, and taking Azalea's arm, she persuaded her to get up from the lounging chair.

On her feet, the girl shook herself with a careless abandon of manner, unheeding the fact that a hairpin flew from her loosened hair, and she dropped the handkerchief, gloves and small bag that she had had in her lap.

"Oh, pshaw," she said, as Bill restored them, "ain't I awful! That's me—dropping things all the time! But I can pick them up myself—don't you be bothering."

She stuffed gloves and handkerchief in the bag, slinging it on her arm. "My, what a vine!" she said, pulling down a branch of the wistaria,—and, incidentally, breaking it off.

"Oh, golly! Look what I done! Just like me! But you've got plenty left." She tossed the broken branch out on the lawn, and then turned to follow Patty, already in the doorway.

"I'm coming!" she said, "lead the way, Cousin, I'll trail you. What a big house! Don't you ever get lost in it?"

"No," smiled Patty, "and you won't as soon as you're used to it. This way, Azalea."

"Hello! *Hello*! This my room?" The Western girl looked at the pretty yellow room as Patty ushered her in.

"Yes, if you like yellow,—if not—"

"Oh, yes, I like yellow good enough. Don't make any diff to me what colour a room is. Nice and big, ain't it? Say, do you care if I chuck some of the lace props into the discard?"

"What do you mean?"

"Why, these here, now, faddly-duds." And Azalea whisked off a little lace stand-cover, swept up an armful of lace pillows, and was about to jerk off the lace bedspread, when Patty protested.

"Oh, wait a minute,—of course you needn't have anything you don't want,—but Janet will take off the spread."

"'Fraid I'll muss it up, hey?" Azalea laughed, "Well. I s'pose I *am* a terror! But honest to goodness I can't stand for those ticklers. They get in my ears!"

Patty sighed. She had grasped the situation the instant she first laid eyes on the girl, but somehow it seemed to be developing further difficulties all the time.

"Now, Azalea," she began, "let me help you get your travelling dress off and put you into your kimono, and we'll chat over a cup of tea. Oh, you don't like tea,—will you have lemonade?"

"Yep. Love it! Plenty of sugar, though."

Patty gave the order to Janet, who had appeared to look after the visitor, and turned back at the sound of Azalea's loud, strident laughter.

"Kimono! At six P.M. That's good. Why, Cousin, I use my kim for a dressing gown, I ain't going to bed,—am I?"

"No, dear. But we'll have a more cosy time, I think, if you get off your travel things and have a refreshing bath."

"Oh, well, I'll take off this rig,—I want to be choice of it, anyway. You have dinner at night?"

"Yes, we always do."

"Well, don't make any change for me, as I said. I ain't accustomed to it, but I can stand it, I guess. Nothing fazes *me*!"

Azalea took off her dress and looked at the skirt with concern.

"Some dusty," she remarked, "but it'll brush off."

"Oh, yes; lay it on that chair. Janet will look after it."

"Brush it, you mean?"

"Yes; clean it and press it properly."

"My land! does your servant do that?"

"Certainly. And leave your street shoes out for her to attend to."

"Oh,—I see! She's a regular outfit! Well, I never had a maid, —but I guess I can stand one."

Janet re-entered the room at this moment, and with an attempted air of grandeur, Azalea flung herself into a low chair, and stuck out her foot to have her shoe removed.

Patty gasped. The girl changed so quickly from independence to apparent helplessness, and yet her manner was so crude and overbearing, that it was doubtful how the maid would take it.

However, Janet was not only a well-trained servant, but she adored her mistress and not for worlds would she have failed in her duty.

Quietly and respectfully she knelt before Azalea and took off her shoes and waited on her as she would have waited on any of Patty's more cultured friends.

"Yes, put on a kimono, Azalea," Patty said, this time in a decided tone, and Azalea obeyed.

Then the tea tray was brought and the two sat together for a time.

Patty was up against a crisis. She had been thinking deeply ever since Azalea's arrival, and she was still perplexed.

Should she try *now* to reform the girl,—improve her manners, or at least her general attitude,—or, should she leave her to her own ways for a time, and trust to her observation of other people to show her her own faults?

It was almost impossible not to correct some of Azalea's ignorant mistakes, but still more difficult to ignore her over readiness to adapt herself to what she thought was the proper behaviour toward servants.

On the latter point Patty permitted herself a word when they were alone.

"Be a little careful with Janet," she said, pleasantly. "She's a bit peculiar as to disposition. A splendid maid, and a most capable girl,—but she doesn't like to be ordered about too definitely. You see, she knows her duties so well, and is so efficient, that it's really unnecessary to give her directions."

"Oh, pooh, she's only a servant. You oughtn't to stand for her airs. Why, our girl at home,—she was a Tartar! But I tamed her. I've a way with them—"

"Please, Azalea," and Patty smiled ingratiatingly, "remember, won't you, that this is my house and these are my servants. I have my own ways of treating them, and I'm going to ask you to work with me,—not against me."

"Dunno what you mean! I've no notion of working against you, Cousin. And don't you be high and mighty with *me*! We'll get along all right, if you meet me half way, but—"

Patty saw her chance. "Good, Azalea! There's my hand on that! We'll meet each other half way, and you consider my wishes and I'll consider yours."

The danger point was passed and Azalea smiled again.

"I want to see the baby," she said suddenly. "I love babies."

"To-morrow, please. She's asleep now."

"Well, I can look at her. I won't wake her. I'll be awful careful."

This interest in Fleurette touched Patty's mother heart, and she consented.

"Can I go this way?" said Azalea, looking at her kimono.

This garment was,—not entirely to Patty's surprise,—a horror of gaily flowered silkoline, but as they would see no one but the nurse, she said, "Yes; come along."

To the nursery they went and there, in her bassinette lay the baby, asleep. She looked like a lovely little flower, indeed, and Patty gazed with adoring eyes at the flushed little face.

"Oh!" cried Azalea, aloud, "what an angel baby!"

"Hush!" whispered Patty, "don't wake her!" and Nurse Winnie stood around in a state of nervous apprehension.

"No, I won't," Azalea said, in such a loud whisper, that it was scarce a whisper at all,—rather a muffled shout.

And then she poked her forefinger into the baby's roseleaf cheek.

"Pretty!" she said, beaming at the child.

"Oh, don't touch her!" Patty cried out. "Come away, Azalea!" for she really didn't know what the strange girl would do next.

"Pshaw! I didn't hurt her. If she's such a touch-me-not, she's no fun at all! But every-body's like that with their first baby! Silly! Fussy! Just ridiculous!"

"I daresay," laughed Patty, determined not to show her annoyance. "But it's time to dress for dinner,—or nearly. Come back to your room,—and—wouldn't you like to take a fifteen minute nap? It might refresh you."

"It would *not*! Take a nap in broad daylight! I never heard of such a thing! Oh, well, if I can't speak to that kid let's go back to my room. I'll skittle into my frock and go down to that flowery, bowery piazza again. I like that."

"What shall you put on?" asked Patty, interestedly, as Azalea made a mad dive into her trunk.

"Dunno. What say? This?" She held up a mussy looking white muslin, trimmed with coarse embroidery and some imitation lace.

"That will do nicely," Patty said, relieved that it was at least white, and not some of the flamboyant effects she saw still in the trunk. "Janet will press it off for you,—it's rumpled from packing. And then you needn't unpack, dear, Janet will do that for you."

"Oh, I thought you told me not to call on the servant for anything!"

"No," Patty said, discouraged, "I didn't quite say that,—here's Janet now. Let her do your hair for you!"

"Do my hair! Mercy gracious! I should say not! I've never had that done for me."

"But I'm sure you'll be pleased with the way she'd do it. Janet is an artist at hair-dressing."

"Nopy! nix on the barber act for little Zaly! I'll comb my own wig, thank you!"

With a comb, she stood before the cheval glass, and twisted up the dark mop into a tidy but most unbecoming coil.

"Don't you *care* how it looks?" cried Patty, in dismay. "Really, *don't* you? And you've such pretty hair!"

"Then if it's pretty hair, it doesn't need any fancy doing," and

Azalea gave a whimsical smile. "There, that's done. Now for my frock."

Janet had whisked the white muslin away, and already had it back, pressed and freshened.

"Lovely!" Azalea exclaimed; "how ever did you do it so quick? Happen to have an iron on the stove?"

"Electric iron," said Patty, briefly. "They're always handy, you know."

"Never saw one. No, Miss Janet,—not that way, it hooks in the back."

At last, Azalea was attired, and looked fairly presentable in her white frock; though having no white shoes and stockings she wore black ones.

"I'd like white ones," she said, apologetically, "but I could only have two pairs so I got black and the ones I wore here."

"Quite right," said Patty, appreciatively; "I'll be glad to get you some white ones. They'd be pretty with this frock."

"Oh, thank you. I'd love to have 'em. Where we going now?"

"Suppose you come to my room, while I dress," Patty suggested, thinking an object lesson in the arts of the toilette might not be amiss.

"O.K.," and the visitor strode along by the side of her hostess.

They *were* a contrast! Patty, dainty, graceful and sweet, was the very antithesis of tall, gawky Azalea, with her countrified dress and badly made black shoes. Her careless air, too, was unattractive,—for it was not the nonchalance of experience, but the unselfconsciousness of sheer ignorance of urban ways and manners.

"My land! what a room," the country girl ejaculated, as they entered Patty's boudoir. "How ever can you live in this fancy place! It's like a picture!"

"It is," agreed Patty, pleased at the comment. "But I love it. I'm afraid I'm too fond of soft lights and pretty appointments, and delicate fragrance."

"Well, you've got it! My land! I'm afraid to move around! I don't want to break anything."

"You won't," laughed Patty. "Sit there, and we can talk while I get into my gown. I do my own hair, too," and she shook down her mop of golden curls, to Azalea's hearty admiration.

CHAPTER VI

TABLE MANNERS

Patty's dining-room was beautiful. She argued that as an appreciable percentage of one's waking hours were spent there, care and thought should be given to its appointment.

The colouring was soft old blue, and the furniture of mahogany. The lights were pleasantly shaded and the sideboards and cabinets showed attractive silver and glass in immaculate order.

"The flowers are in your honour," said Patty, smiling, as they took their places at the table, in the centre of which was a bowl of azaleas.

"Ho, ho! You needn't have done that! I ain't accustomed to such grand things."

"Now, Azalea, flowers on the table aren't especially grand. I think I should have them,—if I could,—if I were eating in the middle of the Desert of Sahara."

"I believe you would," said Bill, smiling at her; "Patty is a flower-worshipper, Zaly. Zaly's the name your mother called you when you were a tiny mite. Tell me about your father? Was he willing to be left alone?"

"Oh,—he didn't mind. What lovely silver you have, Patty."

"Yes; they are my wedding presents."

"Oh, tell me all about your wedding!"

"I didn't have any. I mean, not a big reception and all that. We were married in haste,—so we could have a chance to repent at leisure,—if we want to."

"And do you?" asked Azalea, with such a serious air that the other two laughed.

"I haven't had leisure enough for *that* yet," Bill declared.

"And I don't know what leisure means," Patty said. "I'm busy from morning till night. If we ever get any leisure,—either of us,—perhaps we'll begin on that repentance performance."

But Patty's happy face, as she turned it toward her husband, left little doubt as to her state of satisfaction with her life. Though, as she said, she was always busy, it was by her own wish, and she would have been miserable if she had had nothing to do.

Azalea, as Bill expressed it later to Patty, was a whole show!

The girl was ignorant of manners and customs that were second nature to her hosts, and was even unacquainted with the uses of some of the table furniture.

But this they had expected, and both Patty and Bill were more than ready to ignore and excuse any lapses of etiquette.

However, they were not prepared for Azalea's attitude, which was that of self-important bravado. Quite conscious of her shortcomings, the girl's nature was such that she preferred to pretend familiarity with her strange surroundings and she assumed an air of what she considered elegance that was so funny that the others had difficulty to keep from laughing outright.

She was especially at great pains to extend her little finger when she raised a glass or cup, having evidently observed the practice among people she admired. This finally resulted in her dropping the glass and spilling water all over her dinner plate.

"Hang it all!" she cried; "ain't that *me*! Just as I get right into the swing of your hifalutin ways, I go and upset the applecart! Pshaw! You'll think I'm a country junk!"

"Not at all," said Patty, kindly, "'twas an accident that might happen to anybody. Norah will bring you a fresh plate. Don't think of it."

"No, I won't have a fresh plate. I'm going to keep this one, to serve me right for being so awkward." And no amount of insistence would persuade the foolish girl to have her plate changed.

"Nonsense, Azalea!" Farnsworth remonstrated, "you can't eat that chicken, floating around in a sea of potato and water! Don't be a silly! Let Norah take it."

"No, I won't," and a stubborn look came into the black eyes. But in the meantime, Norah had attempted to remove the plate,—carefully, not to spill the water.

Azalea made a clutch at it, and succeeded in overturning the whole thing,—and the food fell, partly in her lap and partly on the pretty tablecloth.

"Never mind," said Patty, gaily. "Leave it all to Norah,—she'll do a conjuring trick."

And sure enough, the deft waitress whisked the details of the accident out of sight, spread a large fresh napkin at Azalea's place, set another plate for her, and was passing her the platter of chicken almost before she realised what was going on.

"Well, I never!" she exclaimed; "that was *some* stunt! Say, I'm sorry, Cousin Patty,—but I'm a little kerflummixed,—and I may as well own up to it."

"Oh, don't be that!" Patty laughed, carelessly. "Forget the past and enjoy a piece of hot chicken. It's real good,—isn't it?"

"It's great! I never tasted anything like it!" Whereupon, Azalea took in her fingers a wing and, with both elbows on the table, proceeded to enjoy it in her own informal way. But both little fingers were carefully extended at right angles to the others. She glanced at them now and then, to make sure.

Her equanimity restored by Patty's kindliness and tact, the girl lapsed into what was, doubtless, her customary way of eating. She displayed undue gusto, smacked her lips at the appearance of a dainty dish and when the dessert proved to be ice cream, she rolled her eyes ceilingward, and patted her chest in a very ecstasy of anticipation.

It was too much for Farnsworth. He appreciated Patty's patience and endurance, but he knew just how she felt. And it was *his* cousin who was acting like a wild Indian at their pretty home table!

"Azalea," he said,—Norah had left the dining-room,—"who brought you up? Your mother died some years ago. With whom have you lived since?"

"Why,—oh,—only with Papa."

"But Uncle Thorpe,—I remember him well,—was a simple soul, but he was a quiet, well-behaved man. Why didn't he teach you to be more restrained in your ways,—especially at table?"

"Restrained? Oh, you mean I eat too much! Well, I have got a big appetite, but to-night I guess I'm specially hungry. Or else your eats are specially good! You don't mind how much I eat, do you, Cousin Patty?"

Carolyn Wells

"Of course she doesn't," Farnsworth went on, trying to look severe but obliged to smile at Azalea's total unconsciousness of any wrong manners on her part. "But she does care if you behave like a 'wild and woolly,' although she's too polite to say so!"

"Wild and woolly nothing! I've been awful careful to crook out my finger,—and that's the very reason why I upset the tumbler!"

"That's true," agreed Patty, "and so, Zaly, suppose you discontinue that habit. It isn't done this year."

"Honest? That so? I'd be mighty glad to quit it!"

"Do, then," put in Bill. "And while we're on the subject, you won't mind if I go into it a little more deeply,—will you?"

"What do you mean?"

"Well, for one thing, they don't put elbows on the table this season as much as formerly."

"Pooh! I know that! I didn't mean to,—but I forgot. I guess I know how to behave,—if I don't always do it!"

"I'm glad you do, Zaly,—and, listen, dear, you're my relative, you know, and I'm going to ask you to try to *use* your knowledge,—for Patty is too polite to mention such subjects!"

"Oh, I don't mind! Pick on me all you like,—either of you. I suppose there are some frills I'm not onto,—but I'm quick at catchin' on,—and I'll get there, Eli!"

Norah returned then, and the subject was not continued. Coffee was served in the library and the small cups excited Azalea's scorn.

"Skimpy, I call it!" she cried. "And where's the milk?"

"You may have cream if you wish it, Azalea," said Patty, a little tired of smiling. "Norah will bring some."

"Oh, let me get it," and Azalea jumped up. "I remember, Patty, you told me not to trouble the servants too much."

"Sit down!" Farnsworth said, in a tone that made Azalea jump. "Wait for Norah to bring it."

"Oho! *you* believe in making the lazy things work, don't you! What's the use of hiring a dog, and doing your own barking? That's right!"

Patty struggled with her annoyance, overcame it, and making a gesture to Bill to keep quiet, she warded off his angry explanations, and took the situation in her own hands.

"Here's cream, Azalea," she said, as the maid reappeared, "many people like it in after dinner coffee, and you're very welcome to it."

"Licking good!" was the verdict, as Azalea stirred her coffee, and drank the tiny cupful at one draught. "The sample's fine! I'll take a regular sized cup, please."

"For breakfast," smiled Patty. "That's all we serve at night. Are you fond of music, Azalea?"

"You bet! Why, we've got some records that are just bang-up!"

"I remember Uncle Thorpe was quite a singer," said Bill; "do you sing, too?"

"Not so's you'd notice it! My voice is like—"

But the description of Azalea's singing voice was interrupted by the entrance of two young people. Betty Gale and her brother Raymond stepped in at the open French window, and laughingly announced themselves as daring intruders.

"Very welcome ones," declared Patty, jumping up to greet them, and then Farnsworth introduced Azalea.

"You're the real purpose of our visit," said Betty, her charming little face alight with gay welcome. "We adore our neighbours, and they simply worship us,—so we're quite prepared to take any friends or relatives of either of them into our hearts and homes."

"My!" said Azalea, unable to think of any more fitting response, and taking Betty's outstretched hand, with her own little finger carefully extended.

Betty Gale's eyes opened wide for a fraction of a second, then she as quickly accepted the situation, and said, cordially, "I'm sure we shall be friends. And you must like my scapegrace brother, too, if only for my sake."

"At first," supplemented Raymond, as he stepped toward Azalea, "but as soon as you know me better, you'll love me for myself alone,—I feel sure of that!"

"My!" said Azalea again. Her bravado deserted her in the presence of these two merry visitors. They seemed so at ease, so knowing, so carelessly polite, that Azalea felt as if they were beings from some other sphere. The Farnsworths, she knew, made allowance for her because she was a guest in their household, but these people seemed to expect her to be like themselves, and she suddenly realised she couldn't be as they were.

A strange contradictory streak in her nature often made her assume an accomplishment she did not possess, and now, knowing she couldn't chat in their lively fashion, she took refuge in an attitude of bold hilarity, and talked loud and fast.

"I'll love you, if you make love to me good and proper," she said, with a burst of laughter. "But I've got a beau back home, who'll go for you, if he knows it!"

"Oh, we'll keep it secret," returned young Gale; "I'm awfully good at keeping secrets of that sort! Trust me. And it shall be my earnest endeavour to cut out said beau. Meet me halfway, won't you?"

"Yes, indeed, and then some! I'm a great little old halfway meeter, you bet!"

"I'm sure of it!" Gale was laughing now. "Let's go out on the verandah and talk it over."

"Don't trust him too implicitly, Miss Thorpe," warned Betty; "my brother is a first-grade scalawag,—and I want you to be forewarned!"

"There, there, Sis, I'll do my own forewarning. Come along, Miss Thorpe, we'll sit under the spreading wistaria tree."

The two disappeared, and there was a moment's silence, and then Patty said,

"Our cousin is from Arizona, and it's hard for her, at first, to adapt herself to our more formal ways. It must be great out there,—all wide spaces, and big, limitless distances—"

"God's country!" said Farnsworth, who always had a love for his Western wilds.

"Nix!" cried Betty, "I've been there, and it's just one cactus after another!"

"Well, cactuses are all right,—in their place," said Patty, smiling. "They're as much verdure as maples or redwoods."

"Quite different kind of verdure," said Betty. "Now, Patty, I want to do something for your cousin,—right away, I mean, to help you launch her."

"Oh, no, Betty; you're awfully kind, but—"

"Yes, I shall, too. I'm your nearest neighbour, and it's my right. I suppose you'll give her a luncheon or something, first, and then I'll follow it with a tea, or a dance, or whatever you like. There'll be lots of things for her later on, so I want to get my bid in first. How pretty she is."

"You're a darling, Betty," cried Patty, enthusiastically, touched by her friend's kindness, "but,—well, there's no use mincing matters,—I'm not sure Azalea is quite ready to be presented to society."

"Oh, but your cousin—"

"Indeed she isn't!" put in Farnsworth, "I want you to understand that she's *my* cousin,—not Patty's. And, also my wife's quite right,—Azalea is not ready for social functions,— of any sort. You see, Betty, we can't blink the facts,—she's of the West, western,—in the least attractive sense. I'm fond of my home, and unashamed of my people, but all the same, I'm not going to have Patty embarrassed by the ignorance and awkwardness of an untutored guest. And so here's where I set my foot down. We accept no invitations for Azalea until we think she is in trim to make a correct appearance in society."

"Oh, Cousin Bill, I overheard you and I think you're just horrid!" Azalea came running back into the room, while Raymond Gale followed, evidently in a dilemma how to act.

"Cousin Patty would let me go, I know, and I *want* to go to Miss Gale's to a party! Just because I upset a glass of water at dinner, you're mad at me! It isn't fair! I think you're real mean!"

The girl went up to Farnsworth and almost scowled at him as she awaited his response.

But he looked at her steadily,—even sternly.

"Of course it must be as Patty says," he told her, at last, "but I will say, Azalea, that I'm surprised at you—"

"Why should you be surprised at me? You invited me to come and see you. If I'm not good enough to visit you, I'll go home again. You didn't ask me any questions,—you just said come along,—and I came. I ain't a swell,—like these friends of yours,—but I am your cousin, and you've got no right to scorn me!"

"That's so, Bill," Patty said, seriously; "and here's another thing. Betty has met Azalea now,—she knows just what she is. If she still cares to ask her to her house, I shall approve of her going. I want to do all I can for our cousin, and there's no better way to teach people to swim, than to throw them into the water!"

"Bully for you, Cousin Patty!" Azalea cried, her eyes snapping at Bill. "I'm not so bad as I might be, and I'll do just what you tell me."

"I'm sure you will," agreed Betty, and Farnsworth looked at her appreciatively, feeling a deep sense of gratitude at the way she was helping Patty out.

"It seems hard on you, Azalea," he went on, "to talk of you like this,—as if you were not present,—but it is so. You need, —I'm not going to hesitate to tell you,—you need a thorough training in matters pertaining to polite society. Unless you are willing to accept our teachings and do your best to profit by them,—I am going to send you back home! For much as I want to be kind and helpful to my young cousin,—I will not even try, if it makes my wife any trouble or embarrassment."

"Oh, pshaw, Little Billee,—leave Azalea to me,—I can manage her."

"You can't, Patty, without her cooperation and willingness. Will you promise those, Azalea?"

"Sure I will! I'm a great little old promiser,—I am!"

"And will you keep your promises?"

"You bet! I don't want to go home when I've just got here! And if my learning things is my meal ticket,—then I'm ready to learn."

Farnsworth sighed. He had had, as yet, no chance to talk to Patty alone, since their misfit visitor had arrived. He had been firmly resolved to send her home again,—until now, that Patty and Betty seemed willing to take her in hand. If they were, it would be a great injustice to the Western girl not to give her the chance to learn refinement and culture from those two who were so well fitted to teach her.

And, anyway,—he continued to muse,—perhaps Azalea's worst faults were superficial. If she could be persuaded to amend her style of talk and her *gauche* manners, perhaps she was of a true fine nature underneath. His Uncle,—so-called,—and his Aunt Amanda, he remembered as kindly, good-hearted people, of fair education, though lacking in elegance.

"Oh, don't take it so seriously," cried the vivacious Betty, as she noted Farnsworth's thoughtful face: "leave the little girl to us for a few weeks,—and you will be surprised at the result! You'll do just as I tell you,—won't you, Azalea?"

"If you tell me the same as Cousin Patty," was the reply, and the strange girl gave Patty a look of loyalty and admiration that won her heart.

"That's right, Zaly, dear," Patty cried, "you're my girl, first, last and all the time! And we'll both do as Betty says,—because she knows it all! She knows lots more than I do."

"Indeed I do!" and the saucy Betty laughed. "Well, then, I'll arrange for a dance for Azalea very soon. Do you dance?"

"I don't know," replied Azalea, "I never tried."

CHAPTER VII

MYSTERIOUS CALLERS

Big Bill Farnsworth came into the nursery, where Patty was playing with the baby. It was the nurse's luncheon hour, and Patty always looked after Fleurette then.

"Take her, Daddy," Patty cried, holding up the soft, fragrant little bundle of happy humanity, and Farnsworth grasped the child in his strong careful way, and tossed her up high above his head.

The baby laughter that followed proved Fleurette's delight in this performance, and she mutely insisted on its repetition.

"Azalea does that," said Patty, in a troubled tone, "she is strong and very athletic, I know, but I can't bear to see anybody toss baby around but you."

"No; Azalea oughtn't to do it,—she is strong, but she isn't careful enough. Don't allow it, Patty."

"I do forbid it, but she comes in here when I don't know it, —or she picks baby out of her carriage, Winnie says, and tosses her clear up and catches her again."

"I'll speak to her about it; why, she'll drop the child some day! She must not do it!"

"I wish you would speak to her," Patty sighed. "Azalea is really a trial. I don't know what to do with her. Sometimes she is so sweet and docile that I think I'm teaching her to be a civilised person, and then she flies off at a tangent and she's as unruly and intractable as she was at first."

"How long has she been here now?"

"Nearly a month. I've tried and Betty has tried,—and, yes, Azalea has tried herself,—but we can't seem to—"

"Camouflage her!"

"That's just it! I want her to look like the background she's against here,—and she doesn't!"

"I should say not! Last night at dinner she threw herself back in her chair and yawned openly—"

"Openly! It was all of that! I saw her,—across the table through the flowers. And, Billee,—she's queer—that's what she is, —queer!"

"Have you noticed that, too? Yes, she *is* queer,—here take this Little Flower. She's nearly asleep."

"So she is,—give her to me,—there, there, mudder's pressus, —petty poppity,—yes, she's queer!"

"Who? Fleurette?"

"You know very well I don't mean Fleurette! I mean that Pride of the West,—that stranger within our gates,—that thorn in the flesh,—that awful Azalea!"

"Meaning me?" and Azalea herself popped her head in at the nursery door.

"Yes," replied Farnsworth, imperturbably, "meaning you.

Come in, Azalea, I want to speak to you. When have you heard from your father?"

"Let me see—about a week ago, I think."

"Will you show me the letter?"

"Why, how inquisitive you are! What do you want to see it for?"

"I'd like to read it. I suppose it isn't distinctly a private letter."

"N-no, of course not. But, the truth is,—I haven't got it."

"What did you do with it?"

"I—I tore it up."

"Was it unpleasant?"

"No, but as I had answered it,—I didn't need to keep it."

"What was in it? Tell me,—in a general way."

"Oh,—it said—he hoped I was well,—and he—he hoped you were well,—and—"

"And he hoped Patty was well! and he hoped the baby was well,—yes,—and after those polite hopes, what else did he say?"

"Why,—why, I don't know,—I guess that was about all."

"Oh, it was! Why didn't he tell you something about himself? What he was doing,—or going to do?"

"I don't know. Papa isn't very much of a letter writer."

"Well, he used to be! It was his special forte. I've had letters from him a dozen pages long. I don't believe he's outgrown his bent of letter writing. Now, listen, to this, Azalea, the next letter you get from him, I want you to show it to me, see? If there's anything in it you don't want me to know about, cut that out,—but show me at least the beginning and the ending,—and a part of a page. You hear me?"

"Of course I hear you,—not being deaf! And I'll show you the letter,—if I think of it."

"You'll think of it,—I'll see to that, myself. You ought to get one soon, oughtn't you?"

"No,—I haven't answered his last one yet."

"Why, you just said you had!"

"Oh, I meant the one before the last—"

"You meant nothing of the sort. And, mind you, Azalea, this is a direct command,—you *must* show me his next letter."

"I won't take commands! How dare you? You have no right to order me about so. I hate you!"

"Don't talk so, Zaly," Patty said, gently. "Cousin Bill isn't asking anything out of the way. There's no reason you shouldn't show him your father's letter,—in part, at least,—is there now?"

"N—no,—but I don't want to."

"Of course you don't," put in Bill, "and for a very good reason!"

"What reason?" cried Azalea, her black eyes flashing.

"You know as well as I do."

"I don't!"

"Very well, say no more about it now,—only remember I want to see the next one."

Azalea flounced out of the room, very angry, and muttering beneath her breath.

"What in the world, Little Billee, are you getting at?" asked Patty, as she cuddled Fleurette into her shoulder.

"There's something queer, Patty, something very queer about that girl!"

"You've oft repeated that assertion, Sweet William,—just what do you mean by it?"

"What I say, Faire Ladye! There's something rotten in the state of Denmark,—there is that!"

"But why are you so anxious to see her father's letters?"

"They're part of the queer element. Have you ever seen her get one,—or read one from him?"

"Not that I definitely remember; but she may easily have read them right before me, and I not have known it."

"But wouldn't she be likely to read a word or two,—or deliver some polite message he might send?"

"I should think so,—but she never has."

"That's the queerness."

"Oh, do tell me, dear, what you're getting at! Do you think Mr. Thorpe is dead,—and she never told us? There'd be no sense in that!"

"Not a bit! It's something queerer than that."

"Do you think he's married again?"

"Queerer than that."

"Will-yum Farnsworth, if you don't tell your own wife what you mean, I'll never speak to you again! There!"

"At risk of that awful condition of things, I won't tell you just yet. But you do this. Here's something you can do toward solving the mystery,—and I can't. Find out for sure,—don't ask her, but see for yourself,—if Azalea gets a letter from Horner's Corners addressed in a big, bold Spencerian hand. I remember Uncle Thorpe's handwriting perfectly, and it's unmistakable. I've not seen it since Azalea came."

"Goodness, do you call it a mystery?"

"I do, indeed. You'll find out it's a pretty startling mystery, or I miss my guess."

"Well, Azalea is a handful, I admit, but I think she's good at heart, and she is devoted to my booful little Fleury-floppet! My own Dolly-winkums,—who looks prezackly like her Daddy-winkums!"

"Patty, you'll go to the lunatic asylum some day, if you let yourself talk such gibberish!"

"Listen to him, Baby mine, my flubsy-dubsy,—my pinky-poppy-petal, listen to your dreadful Dads! Isn't he the—"

"The what?" and Farnsworth strode across the room and took his wife and child both into his big bear-like embrace.

"The dearest, sweetest man in the world!" Patty said, laughing but nearly smothered in his arms.

"All right, you're excused," and he let them go.

Nurse Winnie came then and took Fleurette, and the two elder Farnsworths went downstairs together.

They heard voices on the wistaria porch, and soon saw that Azalea was entertaining two guests.

They were strangers, and not very attractive looking people.

"Shall we step out there?" Farnsworth asked.

"No," decreed Patty; "let her alone. It's probably those people she picked up on the train coming here. She has spoken of them to me. Don't let's go out, or we may have to invite them to stay to dinner,—and judging from this long distance view of them, I don't care specially to do so."

"No. I don't either; the man looks like a drummer and the woman like a—"

"A chorus girl!" said Patty, after one more peep at the stranger.

Leaving Azalea to entertain her friends without interruption they went out on a porch on the other side of the house. And soon Raymond Gale sauntered over from his home next door and joined them there.

"Some strong-arm, your Azalea guest," he said, in the course of conversation.

"Yes," agreed Patty, a little shortly.

"She was over in our gym, this afternoon, and she put up as fine an exhibition of stunts as I've seen in a long time."

"What sort of stunts?" asked Bill.

"All sorts, from lariat or lasso work to handsprings and ground and lofty tumbling. That girl's been trained, I tell you!"

"Trained in a school?"

"No: her work is more as if self-taught,—or coached by a cowboy. She hails from Arizona, doesn't she?"

"Yes. Here she is now; I hear you're an athlete, Zaly."

"Only so-so," the girl replied, half-absently.

"Have your friends gone?" asked Patty.

"Yes."

"I recognised them," began young Gale: "they were—"

Azalea turned to him quickly. "Don't you say who they were!" she cried, emphatically. "I don't want you to! Don't you dare mention their names! It's a secret!"

"Oh, all right, I won't. Don't take my head off!" Ray Gale laughed carelessly, and pretended to be afraid of the excited girl.

"Why, why, Zaly," said Patty, "who can your friends be that you won't tell their names? I'm surprised!"

"Their names are—are Mr. and Mrs. Brown," said Azalea, with a defiant look at Raymond, who merely opened his eyes wide and said nothing.

It was quite evident that Brown was *not* the name of the people who had called on Azalea, and Patty could not imagine what reason there could be for the girl to tell such a falsehood.

"Is that the right name, Gale?" asked Bill, briefly.

But Raymond Gale only shook his head.

"Miss Thorpe says so," he replied, "surely she ought to know."

The subject was dropped and not resumed until after Gale had gone home.

Then Farnsworth asked Azalea who her friends were who had called.

"I told you they were Mr. and Mrs. Brown," she said, glibly. "I met them on the train coming from the West, and we got quite well acquainted."

"But their name is *not* Brown," Bill said, quietly, "tell me what it is,—or, tell me *why* you don't want to divulge it."

"It *is* Brown," persisted Azalea, but the way she spoke and the way her eyes fell before Farnsworth's steady gaze, belied her words.

"I'm sorry, but I can't believe you," he said.

"I can't help that," she returned, pertly, and ran away to her own room.

"What's she up to now?" said Patty.

"Part of the queerness," Bill vouchsafed, and said no more about it.

*   *   *   *   *

The next day, Azalea went to her room directly after breakfast, and, locking the door, remained there all the morning.

At luncheon she was quiet, and absent-minded, and as soon as the meal was over she went back to her room.

It was nearly five o'clock, when Patty, puzzled at such actions, tapped at Azalea's door.

"What's the matter, dear?" she called, through the closed door, as there was no response to her knock.

"Nothing; let me alone!" came Azalea's impatient voice.

"Are you ill? Don't you feel well?"

"Let me alone. I'm all right." The tone was ungracious, and there was no mistaking the import of her speech, so Patty went away.

At dinner time Azalea appeared. She wore the same frock she had worn all day, and Patty looked at her in amazement. Apparently she had been working hard at something. Her hair was rumpled, her collar awry, and her whole appearance untidy and unpresentable.

"Have you been busy?" Patty said; "couldn't you get time to dress?"

"Forgot it!" muttered Azalea. "Sorry. Shall I go back and dress?"

Patty hesitated. It would, of course, delay dinner, which was already announced,—and, too, in Azalea's present state of pre-occupation, she might fall to work again, and not come to dinner at all.

So Patty said, "No, come as you are," and she gave Azalea's hair a touch, and pulled her collar straight.

Farnsworth watched the "queer" girl all through dinner. Azalea had improved somewhat in manners, though her notions of table etiquette still left much to be desired.

To-night she was unlike herself. She answered in monosyllables when spoken to, and paid no attention to the conversation of the others.

"I expect my friend Elise Farrington to-morrow," said Patty; "I'm sure you'll like her, Azalea."

"Will she like me?" said the girl, indifferently.

"If she doesn't, it will be your own fault," and Patty took advantage of the opportunity for a word of warning. "Elise is a person of strong likes and dislikes. If you try to be real nice and courteous she will certainly like you, and if you're rude and blunt, I don't believe she will. Do you care, Azalea, whether she does or not?"

"No," said Azalea, calmly, and Patty gave a sigh of despair. What was the use of trying to help a girl who acted like that?

Farnsworth, too, shook his head, and glanced at Patty with a sympathetic smile, and then they talked together to the entire exclusion of Azalea, who was so wrapped in her own thoughts that she didn't even notice them.

Not waiting for coffee, when the others went to the library, Azalea, with the briefest "good-night," went up to her room, and again locked her door.

"What does ail her?" exclaimed Patty, as she and her husband sipped their coffee.

"I don't know,—but I'm going to find out. Any letter from her father to-day?"

"No; I looked over her mail. Oh, it does seem awful, to look inquisitively at another's letters!"

"It's necessary, dear, in this case. There's a big mystery about Azalea Thorpe, and we must solve it, or there'll be trouble!"

"I wish you'd tell me all about it."

"I will, soon. Trust me, darling, I'd rather not say what I

suspect, until I've a little more reason for my suspicion. It's *too* incredible! And yet,—it *must* be so!"

"All right, my True Love. I can wait. Now, listen, and I'll tell you of the marvellous achievement of your daughter to-day!"

And Farnsworth listened with all his heart to the amazing tale of Fleurette's intelligent observation of a red balloon.

The next day Elise came.

"Here I am!" she cried, as she stepped from the motor, and flew into Patty's embrace. "Where's your eccentric cousin I've heard about? But first, where's my godchild? I've brought her the loveliest presents! Let me at her!"

"All right," said Patty, laughing at her impatience, "come right along to the nursery before you take your hat off."

The two went to the nursery, and Patty softly opened the door. But the room was empty.

"That's funny," Patty said, "Winnie always has baby here at this hour. She takes her morning nap about now. Where can they be?"

The bassinette was disordered, as if the child had been taken from it, and Patty looked at it in amazement. She ran around to several adjoining rooms, and returned, with a frightened face.

"Elise, there's no sign of Baby or Winnie anywhere! What does it mean?"

"Goodness! *I* don't know! Did the nurse go down to see her beau,—and take the baby with her?"

Just then Nurse Winnie appeared: "Here's the food, Mrs. Farnsworth," she said, showing a bowl of steaming white liquid. "It's all ready."

"What food?" said Patty, mystified.

"Miss Thorpe came here fifteen minutes ago, and said you ordered me to a make a bowl of prepared food,—that Fleurette was not getting enough nourishment."

"Why, I did nothing of the sort! Where is Miss Thorpe? And where is the baby?"

"I don't know," and Winnie looked as if she thought Patty was crazy. "Don't you know, ma'am?"

CHAPTER VIII

MISSING!

Elise gave one glance at Patty's white, scared face and one glance At Nurse Winnie's red, frightened face, and then she herself began To scream.

"Stop that, Elise!" Patty cried, "it's bad enough to have my baby kidnapped, without your yelling like a Comanche! Hush, I tell you!"

But Elise wouldn't, or couldn't hush. The word "kidnapped" upset any composure she may have had left, and she burst into hysterical sobbing.

"Of course," she said brokenly, between sobs, "she's kidnapped! You and Bill are so—so wealthy and grand—she's just the child the kidnappers would pick out for ransom—and—"

"Don't—don't, Elise," begged Patty, her voice shaking; "I don't believe she's kidnapped at all. It's far more likely Azalea took her out for a ride or something. She's crazy over the baby and she always wants to have her to herself, but, she says, Winnie won't let her."

"And indeed not!" spoke up the nurse. "Miss Thorpe,—she tosses the child about in a way that'd fair curdle your blood! That she does!"

Carolyn Wells

"That's true," said Patty. "You see, Bill pitches baby around just as he likes, and so Azalea thinks she may do the same."

"Then she did do that,—and she dropped her,—and maybe killed her!"

Elise voiced her new theory with a fresh burst of grief, and the idea struck a chill to Patty's heart. She took no stock in the kidnapping theory, for Winnie had left the child with Azalea, who would have fought off a horde of marauders before she let them carry off the little one. No, whatever had happened was doubtless Azalea's doing. But Elise's notion of an accident to Fleurette might come somewhere near the truth.

"Of course that's it," Elise went on, excitedly. "The idea of a girl throwing a baby about! What did she do, Winnie? I mean did she let go of her?"

"Oh, yes, ma'am! She often would throw Fleurette clear up in the air and catch her as she came down."

"She *is* athletic," conceded Patty. "Over at the Gales' gymnasium she does all sorts of stunts. But I don't want her doing them with my baby!" she broke down, and cried piteously.

"Sometimes," vouchsafed Winnie, "Miss Azalea would toss the baby into the bassinette, instead of laying her down. She always pitched her straight in,—and baby liked it! You see, Miss Thorpe was very gentle with the child, and never missed her aim. But I was fair frightened to watch her."

"You ought not to have allowed it, Winnie," Patty said, severely. "Why didn't you tell me, if you couldn't make Miss Thorpe stop it?"

"Miss Thorpe told me you wanted her to do it, ma'am. She said it was good exercise for the child, and,—you know her father does it,—and,—begging your pardon,—Miss Thorpe is even more skilful than Mr. Farnsworth."

"Well,—it's his baby!" defended Patty. "Oh, Winnie, suppose an accident did happen,—and Miss Thorpe hurt Fleurette in some dreadful way,—and—"

"And ran away, in sheer fright!" suggested Elise.

"No: she'd be more likely to run to the doctor's. Our doctor lives near here. I'm going to telephone him—I'm 'most sure Azalea would do that."

Doctor Marsh was not in, but his office boy said he had not had any call from Azalea by telephone or in person.

Patty was quite calm now. Her efficient self had risen to the emergency and she was quickly considering what was best to do.

"I'm going to telephone Bill," she said, as if thinking aloud,— "but first, I'm going to call up the Gales, and see if Zaly could have taken Fleurette over there. You know Azalea is utterly lawless,—it's impossible to imagine what she will do. Oh, Elise, you've no idea what we go through with that girl! She is a terror! And yet,—well, there is something about her I can't help liking. For one thing, she's so fond of Fleurette. If she has hurt her,—well, Azalea would just about kill herself!"

A telephone call to the Gales' produced no information as to the whereabouts of Azalea or the baby. Betty replied that she hadn't seen any one from Wistaria Porch that day, and was thinking of coming over to call.

"Don't come just now," said Patty, half-absently, and then she hung up the receiver without further words.

"Well, I think I'll have to call up Bill," she said, at last. "You see, he's fearfully busy today, with a specially important matter, and he probably won't be in his own office, anyway. And I hate to intrude on a directors' meeting,—that is, if there's no necessity. And yet,—it seems as if I must!"

Carolyn Wells

"Oh, do," cried Elise; "you really must, Patty! Why, Bill would reproach you if you didn't."

So Patty called Farnsworth's office. Bill's business consisted of varied interests. He was a consulting engineer, he was a mining expert, and he was still connected with government work. So, frequently, he could not be found in his office, though he usually left word where Patty could get in touch with him.

But in this instance it was not so. The confidential secretary gave Patty the address Farnsworth had left with him, but when she called that he had already gone from there.

With long-suffering patience, Patty called number after number, hoping to find Farnsworth at some of the likely places she could think of.

But number after number brought no results,—and Patty turned from the telephone in despair.

"Well, Elise," she said, forlornly, "you might as well go to your room, and get your hat off. Come on, I'll go with you,—and I may think of something else to do about Baby. For the present I seem to be at my wits' end."

Of course, in the meantime the nurse and the other servants had searched the house and grounds,—but there was really no chance of finding Fleurette that way.

It was all too certain that Azalea had taken her away somewhere. And it might be all right,—it might be that Azalea had merely taken the child out for a walk. She had been known to do this,—but never before without Patty's sanction. Of late, though, Patty had objected to it because she feared that Azalea might not return quickly enough. Twice she had been gone for two or three hours, and though the baby seemed all right, Patty didn't approve of the performance.

"That's it," she summed up, after telling Elise of this; "you see,

I haven't approved of such long absences and so Zaly just walked off. Of course, she sent Winnie down for the food, in order to get a chance to put on Baby's things, and depart unseen."

"But she told the nurse *you* ordered the food prepared."

"Yes. I may as well own up, Elise, that Azalea is not strictly truthful."

"Why do you have her around? I think she's horrid!"

"Well, you see, *I* got her here. To be sure, she is Little Billee's cousin,—that is, second or third cousin,—once or twice removed—"

"I wish she was removed from here,—once, twice and all the time!" declared Elise. "Bill had no business to inflict her on you!"

"He didn't. He fairly begged me not to invite her here. But I insisted on it. You see, we neither of us had any idea of what she was like. Bill hadn't seen her since she was a baby, and she was different then!"

"I s'pose so! Well, having found out how 'different' she is now, why don't you send her home?"

"Oh, I can't. And, to tell you the truth, Elise, I want to help the girl. She's ignorant and inexperienced, but she has a sort of native quickness and wit, and I feel sure if I could teach her for a while, she could learn to be one of us,—and in time become a fine woman."

"Oh, you philanthropist! And meantime she has run off with your baby!"

"The baby carriage is gone, Mrs. Farnsworth," said Winnie, appearing suddenly. "So I expect Miss Thorpe took baby in that."

"Yes, probably," said Patty, despairingly. "Oh, Elise, this suspense is driving me crazy! If I knew that Zaly had her,—and if I knew nothing had happened, I'd feel *so* relieved. But suppose she did break Fleurette's little arm or leg—"

"Or back!" put in Elise; "you must *not* let her pitch the baby around! It's criminal!"

"But you don't know how deft she is. Why, she's almost a contortionist herself. She can turn handsprings and—"

"I don't care if she's the greatest acrobat the world ever saw! There's *always* chance of an accident! And with a baby, you *never* know. Suppose Fleurette squirmed out of her grasp, just as she—"

"Oh, hush! Elise, you drive me distracted! It *can't* be anything like that!"

"Yes, it can! I hope it isn't, but do let this be a lesson to you, Patty! Don't ever allow that girl to see the baby again,—much less touch her! I think you and Bill must have taken leave of your senses to give her such freedom! Why, you don't deserve to have that heavenly baby!"

"That's so, Elise, I don't!" and Patty broke into a flood of tears. "My little flower! My precious own baby! How could I ever let Azalea touch her? But, Elise, Zaly loves her as much as we do."

"That may be,—and of course, she wouldn't harm the child wilfully. But, as I said, accidents will happen,—and if it's Bill's fault, why,—of course, it's his own child,—and that's different. But Azalea has no business to take chances with other people's children."

"I know it, and if she only brings her back this time in safety,—I'll never let her see Fleurette alone again!"

All that afternoon Patty suffered agonies of suspense. Now she would cry uncontrollably,—and again, she would sit, still and dry-eyed, waiting for some sound of Azalea's arrival.

But no rolling wheels of the baby coach greeted her ears, nor any little crowing notes of glee from her baby's lips.

Several times she tried again to reach Farnsworth by telephone, —but always unsuccessfully.

At last the long hours wore away, and Farnsworth came home.

Patty flew to greet him, and was instantly wrapped in his big embrace.

"Well, Patty-*maman*," he said, as he kissed her, "how's things today? I had to go over to Philadelphia, on a flying trip,—wish I could have flown, literally,—and hadn't even time to let you know. Then, Rollins told me you had called up several times, —so I skittled home to see what it's all about."

His big, cheery voice comforted Patty, and her trouble suddenly seemed easier to bear, with his help near.

"Oh, Little Billee," she cried, "Azalea has run off with Fleurette."

"Good gracious, you don't say! But how much better to have Zaly do the kidnapping than some professional abductors! Hello, Elise, glad to see you! When did you arrive? This morning?"

"No; this afternoon. But, Bill, this matter is serious. Azalea took the baby away, on the sly."

"That's like her! Azalea has sly ways. And more than that,—she has queer ways! It won't do, Patty, there's something wrong, —very wrong,—about the girl. Did she get a letter to-day?"

"No; not this morning. I forgot to look this afternoon."

"What do you mean?" asked Elise, her curiosity aroused. "Do you keep tab on her letters, Patty?"

"Yes; I'm ordered to by my lord and master. He thinks—"

"Never mind, dear, drop the subject now. I've a good reason, Elise, for watching the letters,—not mere idle curiosity. Now, Patty, for details. What do you mean by taking the baby on the sly!"

So Patty told him how Azalea had ordered the baby's food prepared, saying Patty has asked her to do so.

"H'm, h'm,—looks bad. But don't worry, little mother, I'm sure nothing has happened to our Little Flower,—I mean nothing of an accidental nature. Azalea is exceedingly fond of the baby, and I can easily imagine her wanting to take her for a ride this beautiful afternoon. It's perfectly wonderful out! There's a soft breeze and the air is delightful—"

"But why didn't she ask me?" cried Patty.

"Afraid you'd say no!" and Farnsworth smiled. "You know, you've not been overly gracious of late about Azalea taking baby out."

"I know it, but I had my own reasons."

"And quite right you should have. But, don't worry, I'm sure the two wanderers will turn up all right."

Farnsworth's hearty assurance went far to relieve Patty's fears and when Elise suggested a bad fall, he only laughed, and said,

"No-sir-ee! Zaly is a terror, and a trial in lots of ways, but if she had let that child fall, she would have called Patty and Winnie and the whole household for help, and would have run for the doctor herself! She never would have run away! Not Azalea! She's no coward,—whatever other unpleasant traits she may possess."

"That's so," agreed Patty; "and she truly loves the baby. No, Elise, nothing like that happened,—I'm sure. I see it as Bill does, now. It *is* a heavenly day,—and Zaly felt pretty sure I wouldn't let her take Baby out by herself, without the nurse, —and she does love to do that,—and so she sneaked off, and made up that yarn about the food in order to get Fleurette's hat and coat on! Oh, she's a manoeuvrer!"

"Well, I'm glad you both feel that way about it," said Elise; "of course you know the girl better than I do,—as I've never even seen her! but if she's such a strong-arm, I think I'm rather afraid of her!"

"Oh, I imagine you can hold your own against her!" laughed Patty, happy now, since Bill's reassurance of her darling's safety. "All the same, I wish Zaly would come home! It's after six! Come on, Elise, let's dress for dinner, and then that will be done."

They went to their rooms, and soon Patty was all dressed and had returned to her post of vantage on the wistaria porch, to look for the return of the lost ones. And at last, through the gathering dusk, she saw a baby carriage being propelled along the roadway.

"Here we are!" cried a voice, which Azalea tried hard to make casual, but which showed in its quality a trace of apprehension.

"Oh!" Patty cried, and without another word flew down the steps, and fairly grabbed her baby.

The child was asleep, but Patty lifted her from the pillows and gazed into the little face. Apparently there was nothing wrong, but the golden head cuddled down on Patty's shoulder and the baby slept on.

"She's tired," vouchsafed Azalea, "but she's all right."

"Where have you been?" asked Farnsworth sternly, as he came out of the front door.

"Just for a walk," said Azalea, trying to speak pertly, but quailing before the accusing blue eyes fixed upon her.

Patty said no word to the girl, but holding Fleurette close, went at once to the nursery with her.

"She's all right, Winnie, isn't she?" the mother asked, anxiously.

"Yes, ma'am,—I think so,—but she's a little too droopy for mere sleepiness."

"Droopy! what do you mean?"

"It may be nothing,—Mrs. Farnsworth,—it may be only that she's tired out and very sleepy,—but she acts a mite as if she'd been—"

"Been what? Speak out, Winnie! What do you mean?"

"Well,—she acts to me like a baby that's had something soothing—some drops, you know."

"Something to make her sleep?"

"Yes, ma'am."

"Oh, nonsense! Miss Thorpe couldn't give her anything like that! And why would she? Don't you make any mistake, Winnie, Miss Thorpe adores this baby!"

"I know it, she does, Mrs. Farnsworth, but all the same,—look at those eyes, now."

Patty looked, but it seemed to her that the blue eyes drooped from natural weariness, and assuring herself that no bones were broken or out of place, she drew a long sigh of relief and told Winnie to put Fleurette to bed as usual.

The nurse shook her head sagely, but said no more of her fears.

Patty returned to the porch where Farnsworth was still talking to Azalea. Apparently he had scolded her sharply, for she was crying, and that with Azalea Thorpe was a most unusual performance. She usually resented reproof and talked back in no mild-mannered way. But now she was subdued and even frightened of demeanour, and Patty knew that Bill had done all that was necessary and further reproaches from her were not needed.

"And another thing," Farnsworth was saying, "I want to know why you have had no letters from your father since I asked to see one,—that was two or three weeks ago!"

"I have had one," Azalea answered, sullenly, "I had one this morning."

"Let me see it," demanded Bill, and Azalea went up to her own room and returned with the letter.

There was no envelope on it, and Farnsworth opened the folded sheet and read:

MY DEAR CHILD:

I received your last letter and I am very glad you are having such a nice time. It must be very pleasant at the grand house where you are staying,—and I suppose you are getting grand too. I am very lonesome without you, but I am willing, for I want you to have a good time and get improvement and all that. Remember me kindly to Cousin William and his wife. I like to hear you tell about the baby. She must be a fine child. I am well, and I hope you are, too. With much affection, from your loving

FATHER.

"Where's the envelope?" asked Farnsworth, as he raised an unsmiling face to Azalea.

"I tore it up."

"Why?"

"I always do,—I never save envelopes. It was just a plain one."

"Address typewritten?"

"Yes."

"All right, Zaly. Here's your letter," and he handed it back to her.

CHAPTER IX

VANITY FAIR

The Farnsworths made no difference in their treatment of Azalea, after her escapade. Bill had scolded her severely for taking the baby away without leave, and sternly forbidden her ever to do so again, and the girl had promised she would not.

Patty had said nothing to her on the subject, feeling that she could best keep Azalea's friendliness by ignoring the matter, and she was trying very hard to teach the girl the amenities of social life.

And Azalea was improving. She behaved much better at table and in the presence of guests. Patty rejoiced at the improvement and, as she took strict care that Azalea should have no opportunity to see Fleurette alone, she feared no repetition of those anxious hours when the baby was missing.

Elise rather liked the Western girl. They became good friends and went for long strolls together. Elise was a good walker, and Azalea was tireless.

One day they had gone a long distance from home, when suddenly Azalea said, "I wish you'd stay here a few minutes, Elise, and wait for me."

"Why, where are you going?" asked the other, in astonishment.

Carolyn Wells

"Never mind, it's a little secret,—for the present. You just sit here on the grass and wait,—there's a duck. Here's a book you can read."

Azalea offered Elise a small volume—it was a new humorous publication, and one Elise had expressed a desire to read. She took it, saying, "All right, Zaly, go ahead, but don't be too long."

Azalea left her, and Elise soon became absorbed in the book.

It was a full half hour before Azalea returned.

"Where *have* you been?" asked Elise, looking up, and then glancing at her watch. "It's half-past four!"

"I know it. That's not late. Come on, let's go home."

Azalea was smiling and in an excited mood, but she looked tired,—almost exhausted, as well. She was flushed, and her hair was rumpled, and her breath came quickly, as if she had been through some violent exercise.

"What *have* you been up to, Zaly?" Elise asked, curiously. "You look all done up!"

"I went for a walk by myself. Sometimes I have moods—"

"Fiddlesticks! Don't try to make me think you had a longing for self-communion or any foolishness of that sort! I know you, Azalea Thorpe! You went off to meet somebody—"

"I did not! How you talk, Elise Farrington!"

"Yes, you did! Somebody that you don't want Patty and Bill to know about. Oh, you don't fool me! I'm not a blind bat!"

"Well, you're way off! How could I possibly know anybody they don't know?"

"You do, though. You had some people come to see you, and the Farnsworths didn't meet them at all."

"How do you know?"

"Patty told me."

"Tattle-tale! It's none of her business if I did!"

"Now, look here! I won't stand for such talk about Patty! You stop it! She's not only your hostess but she's the best friend you ever had or ever will have! She's making you over,—and goodness knows you needed it!"

"And that's none of *your* business! I'm as good as you are, —this minute!"

"I didn't say you weren't! It isn't a question of goodness. You may be a saint on earth compared to me, but you don't know how to behave in decent society,—or didn't, till Patty took you in hand."

"She invited me to visit her! I didn't ask her to have me!"

"Yes, because she wanted to be kind to her husband's people, and you seemed to be the only one available."

"Well, I was. And as I'm Cousin William's only relative, I have a right to visit him as long as I please."

"I don't deny that, Azalea," and Elise couldn't help laughing at the defiant air of the speaker. "I'm not disputing your right to be here. But I do deny your right to say anything whatever against Patty, who is trying her best to do all she can for your pleasure and for your good."

"That's so," and Azalea's manner suddenly changed. "Patty is a dear, and I love her. And that baby! Oh!"

"How crazy you are over that child," Elise exclaimed. "She *is* a dear baby, but I don't see why you idolise her so."

"Oh, I love babies, and Fleurette is so sweet and soft and cuddly! I love to have her all to myself,—but Patty won't let me."

"I don't wonder! Where did you go with her that day, Azalea?"

"Nowhere in particular. Just for a walk in the country. I mean I walked. Baby rode in her coach."

"But you went somewhere. Nurse Winnie insists you gave the child some soothing syrup,—or whatever they call it."

"What! I did nothing of the sort! Why, Elise, I wouldn't do such a thing! I love that kiddy! I wouldn't give her a morsel to eat or drink. I know how careful Nurse and Patty are about that! You must be crazy to think I'd give Baby anything!"

Azalea's honesty was unmistakable, Elise couldn't doubt she was speaking the truth. She began to think Nurse Winnie had imagined the soothing syrup.

The two girls went home, and Elise said no word to any one of Azalea's strange disappearance for a time.

They found Patty in a state of great excitement and interest over a new project.

Betty Gale was there and the two heads were together over a list they were making and they were chattering like a couple of magpies.

"Oh, Elise," Patty cried out, "we're getting up the grandest thing! It's going to be here,—for the benefit of the Summer Fund, and it's going to be Vanity Fair!"

"What? What does that mean?"

"Just what it says! It's a big bazaar,—of course,—and we're going to call it Vanity Fair and sell only gay, dainty, dinky little contraptions, and have all sorts of pretty booths and fancy dances and flower stands, and—oh, everything that Vanity Fair suggests."

"Fine!" approved Elise. "Great name! Who thought of it? You, Betty? I'm for it,—heart and soul! How about you, Azalea?"

The Western girl stood silent. This was the sort of thing that was outside her ken. Though she had been at Wistaria Porch for some weeks now, and had become fairly conversant with the ways of Patty and her friends, this kind of a gay project was to her an unknown field.

"It must be beautiful,—to know about things like that,"—she said, at last, so wistfully, that Patty put out a hand and drew Azalea to her side.

It was this sort of a speech that made Patty feel that she was making headway in her efforts to improve the girl, and she rejoiced to have her show a desire to join in the new project.

"You can help us lots, I'm sure, Zaly," she said, kindly, "and you'll have a chance to learn about it all. There's heaps of fun in a Fair, especially when it's all novel to you. It's an old story to us, but *I* always love anything of the sort. We'll have it here, you see, and it will be a lawn *fete* and a house party and a general hullabaloo!"

"We're making out the committees," said Betty, "and, you'll be here, won't you, Elise?"

"Well, I just guess! You can't lose *me*! I shall be back and forth, of course, but I'll do my share of the work, and exact my share of the fun."

"Fine!" said Betty, a bit absently, as she was deeply absorbed in her list of names.

Carolyn Wells

"Of course," Patty went on, partly to the others and partly as if merely thinking aloud for her own benefit, "there will be all the regulation things,—lemonade well, fortune-telling, society circus and everything, but the idea is to have every one of them just a little bit different from what it has always been before, and have it in harmony with the idea of Vanity Fair."

"The book?" asked Elise.

"No, not Thackeray. I mean, just the idea of the gay atmosphere,—the light, giddy side of life. For instance, let's have a Vanity booth and sell all sorts of aids to beauty—"

"Powder and paint!" exclaimed Azalea, in surprise.

"Well, I meant more like lacy caps and stunning negligees. And yes, of course, vanity cases and powder-puff bags and mirrors and perfumes,—oh, all sorts of foolishnesses that are pretty."

"I know," said Elise, nodding her head. "And we'll have an artificial flower booth,—that's right in line. And people love to buy 'em,—I do."

"And laces," said Patty; "and embroidered boudoir pillows, and oh,—and baby things! Why Fleurette's nursery wardrobe looks like a Vanity Fair itself!"

"Hold on," cried Betty, laughing, "don't go too far. Not everybody is interested in baby togs!"

"I s'pose not," said Patty, smiling. "All right, cut out the Baby booth."

"No," spoke up Azalea, "let's have it. Everybody knows a baby to give presents to. And the little caps and things are so pretty."

"Good for you, Zaly," cried Patty; "we'll have it, and you and I will run it, and Fleurette shall be the presiding genius, and sit enthroned among the fairy wares! Oh, it will be lovely!"

"Yes, do have it," agreed Betty. "It will be a screaming success with Fleurette in it!"

"And if you want such things," Azalea went on, losing her diffidence, "I can get a lot of Indian things from home,—baskets,—you know,—and leather, and beaded things."

"Fine, Zaly!" and Elise smiled at her. "We do want those, —real ones,—they always sell."

They went on planning, all working in harmony, and each full of suggestions, which the others approved or criticised, in frank, friendly fashion.

Then Janet appeared to call Azalea to the telephone, and the girl looked up, surprised. She blushed scarlet, and hurried from the room.

"Who could have called her?" said Elise; "she doesn't know any one you don't know,—does she, Patty?"

"No; but she knows lots of our friends. Somebody is probably asking her to go somewhere."

None of them tried to listen, but the telephone was in the next room and Azalea's voice had a peculiar carrying quality that made it difficult not to overhear snatches of her conversation.

"No," she exclaimed, positively, "I can't do it! I really can't! I'm sorry it didn't go right, but I *can't* do it again! It's impossible!"

A pause, and then, again, "No, I simply can't! Don't ask me— yes, of course,—I know,—but, you see, they said,—oh, I can't tell you now,—I'll write,—well, yes, I'll do *that*!—Oh, of course, *I'll* be there—but the—the other one—no, no, no!"

These remarks were at long intervals and disconnected, but they were clearly heard by the three in the next room, and though no one mentioned it, each thought it a strange conversation for Azalea to take part in.

Patty listened thoughtfully, feeling no hesitation in doing so, for she had only Azalea's good at heart and wanted to know anything that might help her understand the mystery that was certainly attached to the girl.

In the first place to whom could Azalea possibly be talking in that fashion? Moreover, her voice was troubled, and her tone was one of nervous apprehension and anxiety.

At last she returned to the group, and Patty said, pleasantly, "Who's your friend, Zaly?"

"Nobody in particular," and Azalea looked as if that were a question she had been dreading.

"You mean not a particular friend; but who was it?" Patty was persistent, even at risk of rousing Azalea's wrath, for she felt she must know.

"I won't tell you!" Azalea cried, stormily. "It's nobody's business if I answer a telephone call. I don't ask you who it is, every time *you* telephone!"

"All right, Zaly, forgive me,—I *was* a bit inquisitive."

And so the matter was dropped, but that night after Azalea had gone to her room, Patty came tapping at the door.

It was only after repeated knocking that Azalea opened the door a little way, and quite evidently resented the intrusion.

"I'm just going to bed," she said, ungraciously.

"I won't stay but a minute," and Patty insistently pushed her way in. "Now, don't fly into a rage, dear, but you *must* tell me who called you up on the telephone to-day."

"You've no right to ask!"

"Yes, I have, and, too, there must be some reason why you are so unwilling to tell me. Why is it?"

Azalea hesitated. Then she said, "Oh, I've no reason to make a secret of it. But I think you're very curious. It was somebody I met on the train when I came East."

"A man or a woman?"

"A—a woman."

"Are you telling the truth, Azalea?" and Patty's clear, compelling gaze was direct and accusing.

"Well—well—Patty, it's both."

"Those people who called here one day, and you saw them on the porch?"

"Yes."

"What are their names?"

"Oh,—oh, I forget."

"Rubbish! You *don't* forget. Be sensible, Azalea. You're making a mystery of something. Now if it's anything wrong, I'm going to know about it,—if it's merely a little secret of your own,—a justifiable one,—tell me so, in a convincing way, and I'll stop questioning."

"It *is* a secret of my own,—and it's nobody's business but mine."

"Is it a harmless, innocent matter?"

"Of course it is! What do you think I am? A thief?"

"Gracious, no! I never thought you were that!" Patty laughed. "But I do suspect you're up to some flirtation or affair of that sort, and I have a perfect right to inquire into the matter. Why didn't you let us meet your friends that day they called?"

"I didn't suppose you would care to know them. They're not your sort."

"Are they *your* sort? Oh, Zaly, I thought you *wanted* to be our 'sort,'—as you call it. You don't want to have friends Bill and I wouldn't approve of, do you?"

"Oh,—I don't know *what* I want! I wish you'd go 'way, and leave me alone!"

"I will in a minute. Tell me your friends' names."

"I won't."

"Then I shall ask Ray Gale. He knows them,—he recognised them the day they were here, and you forbade him to tell me who they were."

"Then if he knows them, isn't that enough to assure you of their respectability?"

"It isn't a question of respectability,—I want to know why they are telephoning you,—not casually,—but apparently on some important matter."

"That's *my* business. Oh, Patty, let me alone!"

Azalea was clearly overwrought, and in another moment would fly into an hysterical tantrum. But Patty made one more effort.

"Just tell me the name," she said, gently.

"Well—Smith. There, *now* are you satisfied?"

"I am not," said Patty, truthfully. "Good night, Azalea."

She went thoughtfully away, and communicated to Bill the whole conversation.

"She's a queer girl," Farnsworth remarked, after he had heard all about the afternoon telephoning. "Do you know, Patty, that letter which she pretended came from her father,—she wrote herself."

"What?"

"She did; and on my own typewriter,—here in our library."

"What *do* you mean?"

"Just what I say. I knew it, the moment I saw it, for the writing on my machine is so familiar to me, I can recognise it instantly. The tail of the y doesn't print, and there are lots of little details that make it recognisable."

"Are you sure, dear? I thought all typewriting was just alike."

"Oh, no; it is as greatly differentiated, almost, as penwriting,—some experts think more so. I mean, it can't be forged successfully, and penwriting can. Well, anyhow, that letter Azalea showed me, as being from her father, was written on my machine. She had no envelope, for of course she couldn't reproduce the proper postmark on an envelope she had herself addressed."

"But why,—what for? I don't understand."

"I haven't got it all straightened out yet, myself,—but I shall. Another thing, Azalea is a poor speller, and she herself spells *very* with two r's. She did in a dinner acceptance she wrote and referred to me for approval. So, when I saw that word misspelled twice in the letter we're talking of, I *knew* she wrote it,—I mean, it corroborated my belief. Now, Patty, we've a peculiar case to deal with, and we must feel our way. This telephoning business is serious. Of course, Smith is *not* those people's name! She told you a falsehood. We know she is capable of that! Now to find out what their name is. It isn't too late to call up Gale."

Farnsworth took up the telephone and soon had Raymond Gale on the wire. He asked him frankly for the name of the two people who were calling on Azalea when he recognised them.

"Miss Thorpe asked me not to tell," said Gale, "I'm sorry, old chap, but I promised her I wouldn't."

"But it's an important matter, Ray, and a case in which I'm sure you're justified in breaking your promise—"

"Can't do it! Can't break my word given to a lady."

"But Azalea is a mere girl, and a headstrong, ignorant one, at that. She is in our care, and it is our duty to know with whom she associates. Who were those people?"

"Seriously, Farnsworth, I can't tell you. Miss Thorpe asked me definitely not to do so, and I gave her my promise. You must see,—as man to man,—I *can't* tell you."

"I see your point, and I quite agree, in a general way. But, Gale, this is a—well, a crisis. I'm investigating a mystery and I must *know* who those people are."

"Ask Miss Thorpe."

"I have, and she won't tell."

"Then you surely can't expect me to! After I promised to keep her secret!"

"Why should it be a secret?"

"Ask her."

"Well, tell me one thing; is the name Smith?"

"It is not."

"What sort of people are they?"

"Oh, people of—why, hang it, man,—I don't know what to say to you! I refuse to betray Miss Thorpe's confidence, and so I don't know how much I ought to tell you."

"Are they people I would receive in my home?"

"Scarcely! If you mean, are they your social equals, they are not!"

"Then, I ought to know about them, and forbid Azalea their acquaintance."

"Oh, Miss Thorpe doesn't know them socially!" said Gale, and then he said a quick "good-bye" and hung up his receiver.

CHAPTER X

INQUIRIES

The next day Farnsworth made an occasion to see Azalea alone.

"Come for a stroll in the rose garden," he said to her as they left the breakfast table.

"But aren't you in a hurry to go to town?" she objected.

"No, I'm not. Come along, Zaly, I want to talk to you."

Azalea looked embarrassed. She had on a trim linen street suit, and had an air of alertness as if about to start on a trip of some sort.

"I was—I was just going for a walk," she said, hesitatingly.

"All right, I'll walk with you. Let's make it a long hike."

"Oh,—I'd love to, Cousin William,—really,—but I—I've a lot to do in my room, this morning."

"A lot to do! What do you mean? Does Patty make you take care of your room?"

"Oh, not that sort of work. I've got to—to—write letters."

"To your father?" Bill's look was significant.

"Yes—no,—oh, a lot of letters."

"Look here, Azalea, you come out with me for a few minutes, —I won't keep you long." Farnsworth took her arm, and led her gently down the verandah steps and along a garden path.

"Now, my child," he said most kindly, "tell me why you pretended that letter was from your father, when it was not?"

"Oh, yes, it was—"

"Stop, Azalea! Don't add to your list of falsehoods! You wrote that letter yourself on my typewriter, in my library. *Why* did you do it?"

"How do you know?" Azalea turned an astonished face to her inquisitor.

"I recognised the typing. How do you know how to use the machine so well? Were you ever a stenographer?"

"No; I don't know shorthand at all. And I didn't—"

"Stop, I say, Azalea! I *know* you wrote that! Now, tell me why! I can't imagine any reason for it."

The girl was stubbornly silent

"Unless you tell me why you did it, I shall be compelled to think there is some wrong reason—"

"Oh, no, there isn't!"

"Then,—come now, Zaly,—'fess up. Was it for a joke on me?"

"Yes, yes, that was it!"

"No, that *wasn't* it, and you only grasped at my suggestion to evade the real truth! Now, you must tell me. Out with it!"

"Well—you see, Cousin William, you are always asking me why I don't get letters from my father, and—as I didn't get any, I manufactured one to—to satisfy you. That's all."

"No, no, my girl, we haven't got the truth yet. You had more of a motive than that. And, too, why *don't* you get letters from your father? Is he angry with you? Are you two at odds?"

"Yes,—we are. He and I had a quarrel."

"Azalea, you have a very readable face. I know when you are telling me the truth and when you are not. Now, you are ready to grasp at anything I suggest rather than let me know the real facts of the case. So I am justified in thinking it's something pretty bad. What is it, child? Don't be afraid of me. Did you run away from home?"

"Oh, no!" Azalea looked frightened. Then she burst into tears. "Wh-what makes you think I'm doing wrong?" she sobbed; "I'm not,—I'm oh,—I'm all right!" Her air of bravado suddenly returned and she looked up defiantly, brushing her tears aside.

Farnsworth could, as he said, read her face, and he was quite ready to meet her explanations when she was in a docile mood, but this quick return to her pose of injured innocence roused him to fresh indignation.

"I daresay you *are* all right, Azalea, and therefore it will be easy for you to answer a few questions which I must insist on having answered. Who was it that telephoned you yesterday?"

"Oh, that was Mr. Smith."

"His name is *not* Smith!" Farnsworth spoke so sharply that Azalea fairly jumped.

But she insisted, "Yes, it is—"

"I *know* it is not! It was the man who came here to see you one day,—and whatever his name is, it is not Smith! Tell me the truth or not, as you choose, but don't try to insist on Smith!"

"All right, then I choose to tell you nothing, I have a perfect right to have friends telephone me, and I think it shows an ill-bred curiosity for you to ask their names!"

Azalea's would-be haughty face and her reference to ill-breeding struck Farnsworth so funny he laughed in spite of himself.

Azalea was quick to take advantage of this.

"Oh, Cousin William," she said, smilingly, "don't be hard on me. I'm only a wild Western girl, I know, but I'm—I'm your cousin and I claim your—your—"

Azalea didn't quite know what she *was* claiming, but as it was really a cessation of the interview that she most desired, she turned on her heel and walked rapidly toward the house.

"Hold on!" cried Farnsworth, "not so fast, Zaly. Before you leave me, listen to this. I am not at all satisfied with what you have told me,—or, rather, what you have refused to tell me,—and I am going to write to your father, and ask him why he doesn't write to you."

Azalea stood still, facing him, and her face turned white.

"Oh, no!" she cried, in a tone of dismay, "you *mustn't* do that!"

"But I will. There's no reason I shouldn't write to my relative. And I must get at the mystery of this thing."

"Don't do that, Cousin William, don't, I beg of you!" The girl was greatly excited now. Her face was drawn with terrified

Carolyn Wells

apprehension and her voice shook with fear.

"Why not?" Farnsworth demanded, and he grasped her arm as she tried to run away. "I'm going to have this out now, Azalea! *Why* shan't I write to Uncle Thorpe?"

"Be—because he isn't—he isn't there—"

"Is he dead?"

"Oh, *no*! He's—he's—gone away on a—a business trip."

"You're making up, Azalea,—I see it in your face. Tell me the truth about him. Has he married again?"

"No,—oh, no."

"Well, then, where is he?"

"He's—I don't know—"

"You don't know where he is,—and yet you claim you had a letter from him!"

"You say I wrote that letter myself—"

"And you did!"

"Well, then, it was because you insisted on my getting a letter from him,—and—and that's the only way I could think of."

Azalea gave a half-smile, hoping Farnsworth would laugh, too.

But he did not. He said, sternly, "I can't understand you, Azalea. I don't want to misjudge you, but you must admit, yourself, that you're making it very hard for me. Why won't you tell me everything? If Uncle Thorpe disowned you,—cast you off,—or anything like that,—tell me; I'll take your part,— and I'll defend you."

"Would you, Cousin William?" Azalea's voice was wistful; "would you defend me?"

The serious tone disturbed Farnsworth more than her anger had done, and he looked at her keenly.

"Yes," he answered, "but only if you are frank and truthful with me. Now, once again, Azalea, what is the *real* name of the man who called you up yesterday?"

"Brown," said Azalea, and Farnsworth gave a gesture of impatience.

"You're a very poor story-teller!" he exclaimed. "It is not Brown,—or Green,—or Smith. If you had said some less common name, I might have believed you. But your inventiveness doesn't go far enough. When people want to deceive, it's necessary to frame their falsehoods convincingly. If you had said Mersereau or Herncastle,—I might have swallowed it."

Azalea stared at him.

"Why would you have thought those names were right?" she asked.

"Because I should have felt sure you didn't invent them. But when you want to conceal a name, and you say Smith or Brown, it doesn't go! Also, you *look* as if you were fibbing. Why do you do it, Azalea? *Why?*"

"Oh, Cousin William," the girl looked genuinely distressed, "I wish I could tell you all,—I believe I will,—but—no,—I can't—"

Then she shrugged her shoulders, and tossed her head, and her defiant manner returned.

Farnsworth gave up in despair. "Very well, Azalea," he concluded, "I shall write to-day to Uncle Thorpe. I tell you this frankly, for *I* do not do things on the sly. I'm sorry you take the attitude you do, but while I'm waiting to hear from your father, I shall continue to treat you as a guest and a trusted friend. That is all."

Farnsworth stood aside, and let Azalea pass. The girl went back to the house, in deep thought.

She did not go to her room, or write any letters. She dawdled about, started the phonograph going, read a little in a magazine, and seemed generally distraught.

As she sat in the big, pleasant hall, she saw Farnsworth come in, go to the library and sit at his desk writing. Apparently this was one of the days when he did not go to New York. Patty came by—spoke cheerily to Azalea as she passed her, and then went on to speak to Bill.

The two went out of doors together. Azalea jumped at the chance, and running into the library, glanced over the letters Farnsworth had written. As she had surmised, there was one addressed to Samuel Thorpe, Horner's Corners, Arizona.

Azalea didn't touch it. She merely glanced at her wrist-watch and hurried up to her own room.

Sitting there at the pretty desk, she wrote two or three letters, and sealed and addressed them.

Then, sitting on her window-seat, she looked out over the beautiful lawns and gardens. She saw Bill and Patty walking about, pausing here and there. She knew they were selecting places for the booths and stands to be used at the forthcoming Fair.

How happy they were! And how miserable she was! She looked at them enviously, and then again she tossed her hand, in her defiant way, and turned from the window.

At luncheon Azalea was very sweet and pleasant. She talked with Farnsworth gaily, and discussed the Fair with Patty and Elise.

"I'm going to donate some lovely things for the sale," she said. "I've written home for some Indian baskets and Navajo blankets, and some beadwork."

"Good gracious, Azalea," cried Elise, "you'll outshine us all in generosity! I'm making some lace pillows and boudoir caps, but they won't sell as well as your gifts."

"It's very kind of you, dear," and Patty smiled at the Western girl with real gratitude. "I wonder what booth you'd rather serve in, Azalea," she went on. "Of course, you may take your choice."

"When is the Fair?" Azalea asked.

"We're planning it for the middle of July. I think we can get ready by that time."

"I won't be here then," and Azalea looked thoughtful.

"Won't be here! Of course you will! What nonsense!" and Patty's blue eyes opened wide in astonishment.

"I thought I might outstay my welcome," Azalea said, seeming a little confused.

"Nay, nay, Pauline," and Patty smiled at her, "stay as long as you like. As long as you can be happy with us."

But there was an uncomfortable pause, for Farnsworth didn't second Patty's invitation or make any comment on it.

"I'm going down to New York in the car this afternoon," said Elise. "Want to go, Azalea?"

Carolyn Wells

"Yes,—I'd be glad to."

"All right, be ready about three. You going, Pattibelle?"

"No; not to-day. My lord and master is at home, and I can't give up a precious hour of his companionship."

"Oh, you turtle-doves! All right, then, Zaly and I will sally forth to the great metropolis."

Elise was spending a month with Patty, and was going later to the mountains with her own family. They were all anxious, therefore, to get the Fair under way, and to hold it while Elise was still there.

So things were being pushed, and the committees were hard at work. There were innumerable errands to the city, and nearly every day the big car went down and returned laden with materials for the work.

Promptly at three, Azalea was in the hall, and Elise joined her, ready for the trip.

"I mean to mail these in New York," said Elise, who carried a handful of letters.

"I will too," returned Azalea, who also had a number of them in her hand. "Let's take these that are on the hall table,—they go quicker if we mail them in the city."

"All right," said Elise, carelessly, and Azalea, with a stealthy look about, picked up the big pile of addressed mail that lay on the table.

No one was looking and she deftly slipped out from the lot the letter Farnsworth had written to Mr. Thorpe,—and pocketed it.

Going out the door, she handed the rest of the letters, with her own, to the chauffeur, to mail, and then got into the car after Elise.

Away they went, chattering blithely about the Fair, and the enormous lot of work yet to be done for it.

"There are so many working with us," observed Elise, "that it seems a big job of itself to keep them in order."

"It all amazes me," returned Azalea. "I never saw people work as hard as you and Patty do. And you accomplish such a lot! And yet, you never get flustered or hurried, or—"

"That's partly the result of long experience in these bazaar affairs, and partly because we both have a sort of natural efficiency. That's a much used word, Zaly, but it means a lot after all."

"Yes, it does. What's your booth, Elise?"

"It isn't exactly a booth. I'm going to have a log cabin,—a real one, built just as I've planned it, and in it I'm going to sell all sorts of old-fashioned things."

"Antiques?"

"Yes, of the proper sort. Old Willow china and Sheffield plate. Copper lustre tea-sets and homespun bedspreads. And samplers! Oh, Azalea, I've three or four stunning samplers! One is dated 1812. That ought to bring a fine price."

"I don't know about samplers. Of course, I know what they are,—but what makes them valuable?"

"Age, my dear. And authoritative dates. People make collections of old samplers, and those who collect will spend 'most anything for a good specimen."

"I've one that my grandmother made,—at least, I can get it.

Would you like it?"

"Would I? Indeed I would! But you ought to keep that, Azalea. My, what a generous girl you are! You'd give away your head, if it weren't fastened on! No, dear child, keep your grandmother's sampler yourself. Is it a good one?"

"I don't know what a 'good' one is. It has flowers on it, and little people,—queer ones,—and a long verse of poetry and an alphabet of letters."

"And the date?"

"Yes; 1836, I think it is."

"That's fairly old. Not a collection piece,—but a good date. Is it in good condition,—or worn?"

"Good as new. I don't want it, Elise,—that is, I'd like to give it to you. You've been awful good to me."

"All right, Zaly, send for it, and we'll take a look at it, anyway."

CHAPTER XI

THE SAMPLER

Vanity Fair was all that its name implied. By good fortune, the weather was perfect,—ideally pleasant and sunshiny, yet not too warm. Wistaria Porch was transformed into a veritable Fairyland, and it was a bewildering vision of flowers, flags and frivolity by day, and a blaze of illuminated gaiety by night.

It was to last but two days, for, Patty said, they might hope for fair weather for that long but hardly for three days.

It was to open at noon, and all the morning everybody was running about, doing last minute errands or attending to belated decorations.

Azalea had the Indian booth. It was a wigwam, in effect, but it was so bedecked and ornamented that it is doubtful if a real Indian would have recognised it as one. However, it was filled with real Indian wares, and the beautiful baskets and pottery were sure to prove best sellers. Azalea received a large consignment from some place she had sent to in Arizona, and other people had donated appropriate gifts, until the little tent was overflowing.

Azalea herself, the attendant on the booth, was in the garb of an Indian princess, a friend of Patty's having lent the costume for the occasion. It was becoming to the girl, and she looked really handsome in the picturesque trappings, and elaborate

Carolyn Wells

head-dress.

Just before time for the Fair to be opened, Azalea went over to Elise's booth. As she had planned, Elise had a log cabin, and in it she had arranged a motley collection of antiques and heirlooms that were quaint and valuable. It was the design of the Fair to sell really worthwhile things at their full value; and as they expected many wealthy patrons, the committees felt pretty sure of a grand success.

"Elise," said Azalea, as she appeared at the door of the cabin, "here's my contribution to your department. I haven't had a chance to give it to you before." She handed out a parcel, which Elise opened eagerly.

It proved to be a sampler,—old, but in fine condition. It was an elaborate one, with many rows of letters, some lines of verse, and several little pictured shapes. There was a beautiful border, and the signature was *Isabel Cutler, 1636!*

"Oh!" exclaimed Elise, "what a gem! Where *did* you get it? Why, Azalea, this is a museum piece! 1636! It's worth hundreds of dollars!"

"Oh, no," said Azalea, "it can't be worth all that! But I thought you'd like an old one."

"But I don't understand! Where did you get it?"

"It was my grandmother's."

"But your grandmother didn't live in 1636!"

"N—n—no,—I s'pose not. Well,—you see, she had it from *her* grandmother and great-grandmother,—clear back,—you know."

"I see," said Elise, scrutinising the sampler. "It's a marvel, Azalea. You mustn't sell it at this Fair. It ought to go to a museum. 1636! That's one of the earliest sampler dates! I can't see how it's lain unknown all these years. Who had it before you did?"

"Mother."

"Oh, yes,—of course. Well, I'm not going to take it from you—"

"Yes, you are, Elise. I want to give it to you. I've wanted all along to give you something nice,—you've been so good to me—"

"Rubbish! don't talk like that, Zaly! If you want to make Patty a present, now,—give it to her. That would be a worth-while return for her kindness to you."

"Oh, I don't think so much of the old thing as you do. I don't even think it's pretty."

"It isn't a question of prettiness, or even of a well worked piece. It's the date. And this is genuine,—I can see that. But I can't understand it! Why,—I think this border wasn't used until—I must look it up in my book. That's home in New York. But, there's one thing sure and certain! This doesn't get put in with my bunch of wares! Mr. Greatorex may come this afternoon. He's an expert on these things. He'll know just what it's worth."

"Oh, Elise," Azalea looked troubled, "don't take it so seriously. It's just an old thing. You've others here that are far handsomer."

"As I told you, Zaly, it's the age that counts,—not the beauty. Run along to your own booth. I'll lay this aside until I can find out about it. But if it's as valuable as I think it is, you mustn't give it to Vanity Fair,—or to anybody. 1636! My!"

Azalea looked a little crestfallen. Instead of being glad at the unexpected value ascribed to her gift, she seemed decidedly put out about it. She strolled round by Patty's booth. That enterprising young matron had caused to be built for her use a little child's playhouse. It was just large enough for half a dozen children, and would perhaps hold nearly as many grown people. But it had a good-sized verandah and on this were tables piled with the loveliest fairy-like gossamer garments and comforts for tiny mites of humanity. Such exquisite blankets and afghans and tufted silk coverlets and such dainty frocks and caps and little coats and everything an infant could possibly use, from baskets to bibs and from pillows to porringers.

And dolls,—soft, cotton or woolly dolls for little babies to play with, and soft, cuddly bears and lambs. Rattles, of course, and bath-tub toys, and all sorts of infants' novelties.

Patty, happy as a butterfly, hovered over her treasures. She wore the immaculate white linen garb of a nurse, and very sweet and fair she looked. Later, Fleurette was to grace the booth and attract all observers by her marvellous baby charm.

At high noon the bazaar was opened with a flourish of trumpets and a fanfaronade by the band. Farnsworth had given the services of a first class band as his donation, and the musicians made good.

The scene was one of varied attractions. The place itself was lovely with its wealth of flower gardens and shrubbery and the unique and elaborate booths here and there among the trees made a striking picture.

Betty was queen of the soda fountain. A really, truly soda fountain had been procured, and it was attended by white uniformed servitors who were trained to the work, but Betty was the presiding genius and invited her customers to sample her beverages, with free advice as to which flavours and combinations she thought the best.

Raymond Gale was a general supervisor of several of the enterprises.

He had in charge the moving-picture men who had expressed a desire to get some scenes of the gay throngs and were willing to pay well for the privilege.

"You like the 'movies,'" he called out to Azalea, "come over here and get into the game."

"Can't," she called back. "I have to be on duty at my wigwam."

"Oh, come along; the wigwam won't run away. At least promenade up and down once with me."

So Azalea came, laughingly, and the two walked grandiloquently into the focus of the camera.

"And there is a man making phonograph records," young Gale went on. "Come over there, Zaly, and we'll have a joust of words, and record it on the sands of time!"

"What do you mean?" asked Azalea, interestedly, for she had no knowledge of some of the performances going on.

She went with Raymond and found a crowd waiting at the booth where the phonograph man was doing business. His plan was to make a record for any customer who cared to sing, recite or soliloquise for him. Mothers gladly brought their infant prodigies to "speak pieces" and went away proudly carrying the records that could be played in their homes for years to come. Aspiring young singers made records of their favourite songs. One young girl played the violin for a record.

Taking their turn, Raymond and Azalea had what he called an impromptu scrap. A few words of instruction were enough for Azalea's dramatic instinct to grasp his meaning, and they had a lively tiff followed by a sentimental "making-up" that was good enough for a vaudeville performance, and which Azalea knew would greatly amuse Patty and Bill when they should hear the record.

"Oh, what fun!" Azalea cried, "I never heard of such a thing. I want to make a lot of records. I'm going to make one of Baby!"

She ran into the house and up to the nursery where Winnie was just giving the child her dinner. "Goody!" cried Azalea, "now she'll be good-natured! Let me take her, Winnie."

Not entirely with Winnie's sanction, but in spite of her half-expressed disapproval, Azalea took the laughing child and ran back to the phonograph booth.

"Let me go in ahead of you people, won't you, please?" she begged, and the waiting line fell back to accommodate her.

But alas for her hopes. She wanted the baby to coo and gurgle in the delightful little way that Fleurette had in her happiest moments.

Instead, frightened by the strangeness of the scene and the noise and laughter of the people all about, Fleurette set up a wail of woe which developed rapidly into a storm of screams and sobs,—indeed, it was a first-class crying spell,—a thing which the good-natured child rarely indulged in.

Not willing to wait for a better-tempered moment, the man took the record and poor little Fleurette was immortalised by a squall instead of a sunny burst of laughter.

But there was no help for it, and Azalea, greatly chagrined, took the baby back to Nurse.

"Here's your naughty little kiddy," she cried ruefully, handing Fleurette over, but giving the child a loving caress, even as she spoke.

"Thank you, Miss Thorpe, I'm glad to get her back so soon."

And then Azalea ran away to her Indian booth, where she found her assistant doing a rushing business with the Indian wares.

Indeed, everybody seemed anxious to buy the baubles of Vanity Fair. The cause was a worthy one, the patrons were wealthy and generous, and the vendors were charming and wheedlesome.

So the coin fairly flowed into their coffers and as the afternoon wore on they began to fear they wouldn't have enough goods to sell the second day.

Azalea was a favourite among the young people. She looked a picture in her Indian dress and she was in rare good humour. She tried, too, to be gracious and gentle, and committed no *gaucheries* and made no ignorant errors.

"You've simply made that girl over," Elise said to Patty, as the two spoke of Azalea's growing popularity.

Patty sighed. "I don't know," she said, thoughtfully. "There's something queer about Azalea. Little Billee has said so from the first, and now I begin to see it, too."

"She *is* queer," assented Elise, "but she's so much nicer than she was at first. Ray Gale is very devoted to her."

"I know it. I like Ray, too, but sometimes,—think,—he knows something about her that he won't tell us."

"For mercy's sake,—what do you mean? knows something about your own cousin that you don't know!"

"Oh, Zaly isn't our own cousin, you know. But—well, never mind now, Elise. This isn't a good time to talk confidentially."

Crowds of people were constantly arriving, and among them were many of Patty's old friends. Many, too, of her newer acquaintances, who lived in Arden and also in the nearby towns.

Patty was charming and delightful to everybody, remembering that she was in a way hostess as well as a sales-lady.

Fleurette graced her mother's booth with her presence, later in the afternoon, and quite redeemed her reputation for good nature, by smiling impartially on everybody, and gurgling a welcome to all who looked at her.

The little garments and toys of Patty's booth were soon sold out, for they were choice bits of needlework and found ready buyers.

And then one enthusiastic young father wanted to buy the playhouse itself, in which Patty had displayed her wares.

"But I meant to keep this for my own baby!" she cried.

"Oh, you can build another by the time that little mite needs one," the young man replied. "And my youngster is four years old,—just ready to inhabit a ready made home of this kind,"

So the pretty little house was sold, and plans were made to remove it to the purchaser's estate.

So it went. Azalea had many offers for her wigwam, if she would sell it after the fair. She agreed to let it go to the highest bidder, and finally received a fine price.

Archery was one of the pretty diversions, and at this Azalea excelled. To the surprise of all, she proved exceedingly skilful with the bow and arrow and easily won the prize offered. But she magnanimously refused to accept it, and returned it to be competed for over again.

Mr. Greatorex, the expert connoisseur in the matter of antiques, arrived at Elise's log cabin and expressed delight in its construction and furnishing.

The cabin was not for sale, Elise laughingly informed him, as Mr. Farnsworth intended to keep it a permanent fixture on his own grounds. Also, Elise went on, very few things of value were left on her tables,—but she still had one piece on which she wished to ask his opinion.

From a drawer she brought out the sampler that Azalea had given her and passed it over to Mr. Greatorex, without comment.

He looked at it, at first casually and then more closely.

His face expressed mystification, and suddenly he examined the date minutely and then smiled.

"Very clever, my dear,—very cleverly done, indeed. Did you do it?"

"Oh, no; it is the property of a friend of mine,—it was done by an ancestor of hers. You see it's signed and dated."

"I see! Oh, yes, I *see*! But you mustn't try to impose on me, —my eyesight is not yet entirely gone!"

"What do you mean, Mr. Greatorex?" Elise was puzzled. "I'm not trying to impose on you!"

"I hope not, my girl, for I wouldn't want to believe such a thing of you. But you have been imposed upon."

"How?"

"This sampler was worked in 1836, not 1636."

"How do you know?"

"Very easily. Here, you can see for yourself. You see how the figures are made,—ordinary cross stitch. Well, as you know, an eight is worked almost exactly the same as a six, except that it has two more stitches on the upper right-hand side. If those two stitches are picked out of an eight, it turns into a six! Now, I'm sure your young eyes can see that two stitches *have* been picked out in this instance. See the slight mark where the canvas is the least bit drawn? And see, on the back a fresh stitch was necessary to keep the ends from ravelling. It would pass to a careless observer, but to one accustomed to these things the fraud is plainly evident."

"Oh, Mr. Greatorex," and Elise looked sorrowful, "I don't care so much about the sampler being less valuable than I thought, as I do about having to think the friend who gave it to me would cheat me!"

"Perhaps she didn't. Perhaps somebody cheated her."

"No; she told me her mother gave her this, and that she had had it from her mother and grandmother—and so forth."

"Then I fear your friend knew of the fraud,—though perhaps her mother gave it to her as it is now."

"Can you judge if the stitches were picked out recently?"

"I should say very recently. The canvas is faded, of course, but, as you see, the threads beneath where the missing stitches were is quite a shade lighter. Had the picking been done years ago, the canvas would have assumed a uniform tinge,—or nearly so."

"Of course it would,—I can see that for myself. Oh, dear! —Well, Mr. Greatorex, don't say anything about this, will you?"

"Certainly not. But that's a good sampler, as it stands,—I mean as a specimen of 1836 work."

"Yes, I know it is. And yet, oughtn't the stitches to be put back?"

"Probably not,—for they could not be matched exactly—"

"But if it remains like this, everybody will think it two hundred years older than it really is."

Mr. Greatorex smiled. "Scarcely," he said. "You see, my dear, the earliest known dated sampler is one of 1643 which is in the Victoria and Albert Museum, in England. There are but six or seven known in that century at all. It would be remarkable, therefore, to find a work of art that would antedate all collections, and yet show the patterns and style of work common less than a hundred years ago!"

"Oh, I understand,—I've read up on the matter somewhat,— but I'm *so* sorry—oh, I *am* so sorry!"

Elise looked woe-begone indeed, for she realised that Azalea had, in all probability committed the fraud herself, and with a deliberate intention of deceiving her.

Azalea's own ignorance of the whole matter was so great, that it was not surprising that she thought the mere alteration of the date would make the sampler of greater value. But what broke Elise's heart was the knowledge of Azalea's wilful deception.

She thanked Mr. Greatorex for his explanations and, again asking him not to mention the matter to any one at all, she put the sampler back in the drawer and locked it up.

"Sold my sampler yet, Elise?" Azalea asked, when next they met.

"Yes; I bought it in myself," Elise replied. "I wanted it, so I bought it. I haven't paid for it yet, for I want to know what you consider a fair price?"

Elise looked Azalea straight in the eyes, and was not surprised to note the rising colour in the cheeks of the Indian maiden.

"Why—why," Azalea stammered, "you said it was worth hundreds of dollars—you said that yourself, Elise."

"That was before I knew of your own handiwork on the sampler."

"What do you mean?" cried Azalea, angrily.

"Just what I say. To the work on the sampler, you added a bit more,—or rather, you subtracted some!"

CHAPTER XII

AZALEA'S CHANCE

"What do you mean by subtracted some?"

"Now, Azalea, there's no use in your acting like that! You know perfectly well you can't fool *me*! If you really want to know what I mean, I'll tell you. I mean that you picked out two stitches from the eight to make it look like a six. Didn't you, now?"

"Oh, well, if you've discovered that, I may as well own up. Yes, I did."

"And aren't you ashamed of yourself? Don't you think such a deception a wrong and contemptible thing to do?"

"Oh, pshaw, it was only for a joke. Can't you take a joke, Elise?"

"It *wasn't* only for a joke. You hoped you would make me think the sampler two hundred years older than it really is! And you thought that would make it much more valuable. Well, you overreached yourself! There were no samplers made—so far as is known—in 1636. So your trick wouldn't fool anybody!"

"All right. There's no harm done, that I can see. My little joke fizzled out,—that's all."

"No, that isn't all. It has proved you are a deceitful girl! You don't mind telling a falsehood!"

"I didn't tell any!"

"Yes, you did! It's an untruth to pretend something is what you know it isn't! If I had sold that to some unsuspecting buyer, for a large price, you wouldn't have said a word! You'd have let it go!"

"Of course; all's fair at a Fair!"

"Oh, don't try to be funny, Azalea; I'm really angry about this matter."

"Huffy, eh? Well, get over it, then! I don't care! *Some* people like me! Don't they?"

The last question was asked of Raymond Gale, who came walking by.

"Sure; I do!" was the hearty reply. "Who doesn't?"

"Elise," and Azalea pouted at the girl.

"Fiddlesticks!" said Elise, gaily. "Never mind, Azalea, I'll take your joke in good part."

For Elise had suddenly decided that she didn't want to spoil Patty's Fair by having a quarrel with her guest. So, though a good deal perturbed by the sampler incident, she preferred to drop the subject.

Azalea understood, and was glad to be let off so easily, though she felt sure Elise would tell Patty all about it later.

With Azalea, however, out of sight was out of mind, and she walked away with young Gale in a merry mood.

As they strolled along, a man stepped toward them, and raising his cap in a respectful way, asked Azalea if he might have a few words with her, alone.

He had a business-like air, and though polite, was, quite evidently, not a man of social position.

Gale stared at him, and Azalea grew very red and confused.

"I—well—not just now," she said, hesitatingly. "I'll see you some other time."

"No, miss, that won't do," The man was courteous, but decided,—and had a manner that bespoke authority.

"If I'm in the way, I'll vanish," Raymond said, laughing a little.

"Well—if you will—" Azalea looked at him beseechingly. "I'll explain later."

So Gale walked off by himself and Azalea turned a troubled face to the man.

"Mr. Merritt," she said, "I can't have anything more to do with the whole affair. I'm quite sure my relatives here wouldn't approve of it, and I can't keep the matter secret any longer."

"But you *must* come, Miss Thorpe. By a strange coincidence you are greatly needed. Miss Frawley has broken her ankle—"

"She has!" Azalea's eyes sparkled, "Oh,—I don't mean I'm not sorry for her,—I am, indeed! But—"

"But it gives you a chance! A wonderful chance,—and if you can make good—"

"Oh, I can! I will! Shall I come now?"

"No; but you must come to-morrow morning at nine, sharp.

Will you?"

"Indeed I will! I'll be there on time."

"And tell your people about it,—don't you think you'd better?"

"Oh," Azalea's face fell. "I don't know. Suppose they refuse to let me go!"

"How can they? They have no real control over you."

"No,—but I'd hate to go against their expressed disapproval."

"Nonsense! This is your first chance at a career. Don't muff it, now! Why, just your skill at archery is enough to put you over! It's the very place for you! Western doings, riding, shooting, lassoing, all sorts of bareback, daredevil stunts—"

"I know—I know. Yes, I'll be there to-morrow. You go, now,—here comes my cousin."

With a quick glance at Farnsworth, who was approaching, the man walked swiftly away.

"Who is he?" Bill asked, as he came up to Azalea.

"Friend of mine," she answered, gaily.

"What's his name?"

"That's telling!"

"I know it is, and I expect to be told."

"People don't always get all they expect."

"Don't trifle with me, Azalea; I'm not in a trifling mood. Who was that man?"

"Ask me no questions and I'll tell you no lies. Now, now, Cousin William, you know yourself, it's very rude to insist on prying into other folks' secrets!"

"Why *is* it a secret? What possible business can a man like that have with you,—that I can't know about?"

"Why do you say 'a man like that'? He's all right."

"All right is a vague term. He's not one of our sort."

"Don't be a snob! Remember you were born and brought up in the West, just as much as I was. And although you've now got to living high and mighty, you needn't look down on me or my friends!"

"You're talking rubbish, Azalea. That man is not your friend, —he was talking to you on some business matter."

"I'm not a business woman!"

"You're not a woman at all! You're a young girl, and a very silly one,—to have secret dealings with a common-looking man. Now, as your temporary guardian, I insist you tell me all about it"

"'Temporary guardian' is good! Who appointed you?"

"I'm that by reason of your being a guest in my house, and too in view of the fact that you have, apparently, nobody to look after you. Your father has mysteriously disappeared. You've had no word from him since you've been here! So far as I know, you have no other relatives, and so, as your nearest of kin, I propose to look after you,—if you will let me. Don't be foolish, Azalea, dear," Farnsworth's voice took on a tender tone, "*don't* be antagonistic. I want to help you, not annoy you. Why not look on me as a friend, and let me know all you're about? There can be *no* reason why I shouldn't."

Carolyn Wells

"You might not approve," and Azalea looked at him uncertainly.

"Why? Are you up to anything wrong?"

"No," but she spoke hesitatingly, "not wrong, Cousin, but— all the same, you might not approve."

"Tell me, and let me see. If it isn't wrong, I'll promise not to censure you, even if I don't entirely approve."

Azalea's attention was attracted by the man who had lately left her. He stood behind Farnsworth and made gestures that informed Azalea she was not to let his presence be known. So she continued to talk to Bill, but also kept the other man in view.

His procedure was somewhat strange. He pretended to be holding a baby, cuddling an imaginary child in his arms. Then he tossed the non-existent little one up in the air, and pretended to catch it again.

Then he nodded to Azalea. She shook her head negatively and very vigorously.

He nodded peremptorily and insistently. Again she shook her head, and as she did so Farnsworth wheeled suddenly and saw the man.

Angrily, he made a dash for him, but the stranger was agile and alert, and ran swiftly away and out of the grounds to the street.

Farnsworth looked at Azalea coldly. "So you were holding communication with him, over my shoulder! This is a little too much, Azalea, and now the crisis has been reached. Either you give me a full explanation of your business with him, or you bring your visit here to an end. I cannot have you in my house, if you are deceitful and insincere. I stand by my offer; I will listen willingly to your story, and judge you most leniently. I don't really believe you *are* up to anything wrong. But a secret is always mysterious and I hold that you are too young and inexperienced to have secrets from your elders."

"I have nothing to confess or confide, Cousin William," said Azalea, putting on a haughty air. "I refuse to be accused of wrong-doing, when I am not guilty of it,—and I will bring my visit here to an end at once! I will leave to-morrow!"

"Oh, pshaw, Zaly, don't go off so suddenly!" Farnsworth laughed lightly, for he had said a little more than he meant to, and he realised, too, that this was neither the time nor the place to have such a serious talk with the girl.

"Come along now, and have tea with us all in the tea-house," he said. "Forget your bad, cruel cousin's scoldy ways, and as to the mysterious man, I'll trust your word that he's all right."

"Oh, thank you, Cousin!" Azalea fairly beamed now. "How good you are! I'll tell you all about it,—some day!"

So the matter rested for the moment, and the two went to join the merry group around the tea-table.

The Fair drew to a brilliant close. The second evening was even more gay and festive than the first. Everything was sold out,—or, if not, it was disposed of by auction after the time-honoured method of Fairs.

Much money had been accumulated for the good cause, and though tired, the workers were jubilant over the success of Vanity Fair.

"I shall sleep late to-morrow morning," declared Patty, as, after all the guests were gone, the house party started for bed.

"Me, too," agreed Elise. "I'm glad you haven't anybody staying here but us. No house guests, I mean, but just Zaly and me."

"I'm glad, too," said Patty. "You see, I expected Father and Nan, but they've changed their plans and will remain in California another month."

"They're having a gorgeous trip, aren't they?"

"Yes, indeed, but I wish they'd ever get home! Just think, Father has never seen Fleurette!"

"She'll be a big girl when they do see her. She's growing like a little weed."

"Like a little flower, you mean! Don't you just love her name, Elise?"

"Fleurette? Little Flower? Of course I do. The sweetest ever. Does Bill still call you Patty Blossom?"

"Yes, at times. Oh, he calls me 'most any old thing! He makes up new names for both of us every day! Come along, Zaly, you're dropping from sheer weariness. Time for little girls like you to go beddy!"

Affectionately Patty put her arm round the girl, and led her away upstairs.

"Sleep well," she said, as she left Azalea in her own room. "And don't come downstairs in the morning before ten or eleven. I'm sure I shan't. The servants will clear everything up, and Bill will oversee it. I hate the aftermath of a Fair,—don't you?"

Azalea nodded agreement, and Patty kissed her good-night and went off.

But it was only eight o'clock the next morning when Azalea crept softly downstairs. She was neatly attired in a cloth suit, with a fresh white shirtwaist and a pretty hat.

She was not at all sleepy or weary-looking and she went out

through the pantry to the kitchen.

"Please give me a cup of coffee," she said to the cook, who was just beginning her day's work.

She looked in amazement at Azalea, for she had had no orders over night to serve an early breakfast.

"I'll get you something as quick as I can," she said, good-naturedly. "I didn't know you was going to town, Miss Thorpe."

"Just decided," said Azalea, carelessly; "and I don't want breakfast,—only a cup of coffee and a bit of toast. There's a good cookie."

Smiling at the cajolery, the cook bustled about and soon had an appetising little repast ready. Azalea gratefully accepted the poached egg and the marmalade in addition to what she had requested, and in a short time had finished and prepared to depart.

But she did not ask for one of the Farnsworth motor-cars; instead, she walked swiftly out of the gate and down the street toward the trolley line.

She waited for a car and when it came she got aboard and settled down for a long ride.

At last she got out and a short walk brought her to her destination. This was nothing more nor less than a great moving-picture studio.

There were a number of people about, all very busy and intent on what they were doing.

Azalea seemed to be known, for two or three nodded pleasantly to her as she went swiftly along to the office.

There she presented herself, and was received by Mr. Bixby, the man who had one day called on her at Wistaria Porch.

"Well, Miss Thorpe," he said, briskly, "I suppose you heard the news. Miss Frawley has broken her ankle—"

"Yes, I heard that," said Azalea, with a sympathetic look.

"And we think we want to put you in her place,—at least, for a trial."

"I'm glad to try," Azalea said, earnestly. "I'll do my best to make good. But I can't bring the baby again."

"Oh, pshaw, yes you can,—just once more, anyway. But never mind that now. We must see about your own part. You know there's danger, Miss Thorpe?"

"Miss Frawley braved the danger," Azalea said, quietly.

"Yes, and Miss Frawley broke her ankle."

"I know; and I may break mine, but I'll take the chance. I am not afraid,—though I well know that accidents may happen. What was Miss Frawley doing?"

"It was in that climbing scene. You know she climbs the sheer precipice of rock. There are hidden spikes driven into the rock for her feet, of course, but she missed one, and fell."

"I'll be as careful as I can, but I may miss it, too."

"In that case, we'll have to get some one else," said Mr. Bixby, coolly. "Are you ready for work?"

"Oh, yes," and then Azalea was shown to the dressing-rooms.

This was her secret. For years she had wanted to be a moving-picture actress, and she had hoped before she left Arizona for

New York that she might get an opportunity to take up the work. She had expected to begin with minor parts, and hoped by her skill and earnest efforts to attain eminence.

On the train, coming East, she had formed an acquaintance with Mr. Bixby and his wife, who were in the business. As their studio was not far from the Farnsworth home, Azalea had made plans with them to engage in the work.

She had carried out these plans, and had been over to the studios several times, taking parts in which they needed a substitute.

She had done so well and had shown such promise that Mr. Bixby urged her to become a regular actress in his company.

But Azalea was so uncertain as to how Patty and Bill would regard such a move on her part, that she had so far kept the matter to herself.

Then, when the star actress had met with an accident, and the management had concluded to offer Azalea her place, it was a great chance for the girl.

She had come over this morning to give it a trial, entirely at sea as to her subsequent attitude toward the Farnsworths.

She thought she would be guided by circumstances as to whether she would confide all to them, or whether she would continue her secrecy as to her movements.

Mrs. Bixby attended to her in the dressing-room. All of Miss Frawley's costumes, it was found, could be altered to fit Azalea.

As one in a dream, the girl stood to be fitted, while seamstresses and modistes hovered about her.

Then she was informed that the work that day would be only rehearsing and the pictures would not actually be taken until her costumes were ready.

Submissively she did exactly as she was told, and so well did she act the parts assigned her, that Mr. Bixby expressed hearty approval.

Azalea was there nearly all day, and when at last she turned her face homeward, a great dismay seized her.

"What's the matter, child?" asked kindly Mrs. Bixby, who was saying good-bye.

"Oh, I don't know what to do!" Azalea was tempted to tell the director's wife all her troubles.

But Mrs. Bixby was a busy lady, and she said, "Not now, dearie. You skittle home, and to-morrow maybe I can take a couple hours off to hear your tale of woe. You know you've already told me your swagger relatives would throw a fit if they knew what you were up to. Well, I guess it's about fit time!"

Azalea disliked her style of speech, but Mrs. Bixby was kind hearted, and she had hoped to have her for a confidante. However, there was no chance then, for Mrs. Bixby hustled her off to the trolley-car, and Azalea went home to Wistaria Porch.

CHAPTER XIII

"STAR OF THE WEST"

All the way home Azalea wondered how she would be received.

Both Patty and Bill were somewhat suspicious of her and would naturally question her as to where she had been all day. She was tempted to tell them the whole truth and throw herself on their mercy, and but for one thing she would have done so. This was the fact that she had previously taken the baby, Fleurette, over to the studios and had used the child in the pictures.

This she felt quite sure the Farnsworths would not forgive.

Azalea would not have done it, if it had occurred to her at first how the parents would resent such use of their child. But Mr. Bixby had needed a very young baby in a certain picture and Azalea, anxious to please, had offered to bring Fleurette over. She was herself so devoted to the little one and so careful of her, she felt no fear of any harm coming to her. Nor did it, for the infant was good and tractable, and did all that was required of her without any trouble. However, little was required except for her to coo and gurgle in one scene, and to lie quietly asleep in another.

But there was one more short scene where Azalea had to rescue the baby from a burning house. To be sure the flames were artificial and there was no danger from the fire, but the baby

Carolyn Wells

was thrown from an upper window, and caught by Azalea, who stood down on the ground.

So accustomed was Fleurette to being tossed about, and so familiar to her was the frolicking with Azalea that she made no objections and was a most delightful addition to the picture.

But something happened to the film, and the director was most anxious to take the scene over again.

Azalea, however, positively refused to take Fleurette again to the studio. She knew how she would be censured, should it be found out, and now Nurse Winnie and the two Farnsworths, as well as Elise, were all watching for anything mysterious that Azalea might do.

She felt almost as if she were living over a slumbering volcano, that might at any moment blow her up. For Elise, she felt sure, would not keep the sampler incident to herself, and if Farnsworth heard of it he would be newly angry at that deception.

So Azalea's delight at her success with the moving-picture company was very much tempered with dismay at her position in the Farnsworth household.

She was almost tempted to run away from them altogether and shift for herself.

Indeed, she practically decided, as she rode in the trolley-car, that if they were hard on her when she reached home, she *would* run away. Of a wayward disposition and without really good early training, Azalea thought only of herself, and selfishly desired her own advancement without thought or regard for other people.

But, to her pleased surprise, when she entered the gate she heard gay voices on the verandah, and knew that guests were there,—and several of them.

Unwilling to meet them in her street clothes, she slipped around to the back entrance and went in at the servants' door.

"I don't want to appear until I can dress," she explained to the cook, and went upstairs by a back way.

Half an hour later, a very different looking Azalea went down the front staircase and out onto the porch.

She wore a becoming dress of flowered organdie, with knots of bright velvet, and her pretty hair was carefully arranged.

Smiling and happy-looking, she met the guests and greeted them with a graceful cordiality.

"Where have you been?" cried Elise, but Azalea ignored the question and quickly spoke to some one else.

Mona and Roger Farrington were there, and Philip Van Reypen and Chick Channing. This quartette had motored up from New York to dine, and Patty had already persuaded them to say they would stay over night.

"I'm crazy for a house party," she said, "haven't had one for 'most a week! Oh, yes. I've a couple of house guests, but I mean a real party. Let's make it a week-end, and have lots of fun!"

The visitors were entirely willing, and after telephoning home for additional apparel, they settled down to enjoy themselves.

As they hadn't much more than accomplished this settling when Azalea arrived, there was no comment made on her absence all day.

In fact, Patty rather forgot about it, in the multitude of her conferences with the housekeeper and the maids.

Farnsworth said nothing in the presence of the guests, and

Elise, after her first exclamation, subsided.

In fact, Elise was more interested in the society of Channing and Van Reypen than in the mystery of Azalea's disappearances.

Betty and Ray Gale had been telephoned for, and they came gladly, so that at dinner there was quite a big party.

"You certainly are a great little old hostess, Patty!" exclaimed Roger Farrington, as they seated themselves at table. "I liked you heaps as a girl, but as mistress of a fine house you are even more charming."

"Thank you, Sir Hubert Stanley!" smiled Patty; "and I'm glad to admit that I learned a lot about managing a house from your gifted wife. Do you remember, Mona, how we kept house down at 'Red Chimneys'?"

"Indeed I do!" Mona answered, "what fun we had that summer!"

"I'll subscribe to that!" declared Farnsworth, "for it was then and there that I met the lady who is now my wife! And,—I kissed her the moment I saw her!"

"Oh, Cousin William!" cried Azalea, "did you really? What *did* she say?"

"Flew at me like a small cyclone of wrath! But as I had mistaken her for my cousin Mona, she couldn't hold me very guilty."

"Yes! A lot Patty looks like me!" said Mona, who was a dark-haired beauty.

"But I didn't see her face," pleaded Bill; "I just saw a girl on the verandah of your house, Mona, and I took it for granted it was you!"

"It's all ancient history," said Patty, laughing. "And, to tell the truth, I'm glad it happened,—for otherwise, I mightn't have become interested in—Mona's cousin."

"Then I bless my mistake!" said Farnsworth, so fervently that Patty shook her head at him.

"Mustn't talk so before folks," she said, reprovingly. "Now, people all, what shall we do with this lovely evening? It's moonlight, so any who are romantically inclined can ramble about the place, and flirt in the arbours,—while those who prefer can play bridge or—the piano. Or just sit and chat."

"Me for the last!" cried Mona. "I've oceans to talk about with you, Patty. Can't we play all by ourselves for a little while?"

"Certainly," said Patty, as she rose from the table. "Mona and I are going to sit on the wistaria porch and gossip for half an hour. After that, we're all going to dance,—and maybe sing."

"Good enough programme," agreed Van Reypen. "For one half-hour, then, each may do as he or she wishes!"

"Yes, if you all promise to be back here in half an hour."

"Make it an hour, Patty," laughed Elise, who had her own plans.

"All right," said Patty, carelessly, who cared only that her guests should enjoy themselves.

"I want to tell you something," Mona said, as she and Patty at last were alone on the porch. "Who *is* Azalea?"

"I call that asking, not telling," laughed Patty; "however, I'll reply. She is Bill's cousin,—not first cousin, but the daughter of his father's cousin. So you see,—a distant cousin. Why?"

"I'll tell you why. Roger and I go to the 'movies' sometimes, —and in a picture, the other night, we saw Azalea."

"Saw Azalea! You mean some one who looked like her."

"No; Azalea Thorpe herself! Roger and I both knew her at once. And it was quite a new picture,—taken recently, I mean. Did you know she did such things?"

"No, and I can't think she does. It must have been only a remarkable resemblance, Mona."

"No, Patty. We're positive. And, too, she was doing Wild West stunts,—riding bareback, shooting, throwing a lariat, —all those things,—and Azalea can, you know."

"Yes, I know; and there *is* something queer going on. It may be that when Azalea goes off for a day or part of a day, that's where she goes. But I can hardly believe it. And why does she keep it so secret?"

"I suppose she thinks you and Bill wouldn't approve."

"And we certainly would *not*! I don't think it can be possible, Mona. But don't say anything to anybody,—not even to Little Billee,—until I can talk to Azalea, myself. I can do lots with her, alone, but not if anybody else is present."

"Where is she now?"

"Gone for a moonlight stroll with Phil. He's decidedly taken with her."

"Yes, I know it. He said so on the way up here. He thinks she's a fine girl—and he admires those careless, unconventional ways of hers."

"Well, I don't," Patty sighed. "I like Azalea for lots of things, —she's good company and kind-hearted,—and she's devoted to Baby,—but I *can't* like those free and easy manners! But she's a whole lot better than when she first came! Then she was *really* a wild Indian! I've been able to tone her down a little."

"You've done wonders for her, Patty. She ought to be very grateful."

Patty made a wry face. "No, she isn't grateful. People never are grateful for that sort of thing. And she doesn't even *know* she's different! I've had to train her without her own knowledge! But she's chameleon-like, in some ways, and she picks up a lot just from being with mannerly people."

"She does indeed! She's quite correct now,—in her actual doings. It's only in some burst of enthusiasm that she oversteps the bounds of propriety. Well, that's all. I thought I'd tell you,—for it isn't right that you shouldn't know. And there's no mistake. There's only one Azalea Thorpe."

"Was her name on the programme?"

"No; she didn't have a star part,—not even a named part. She was one of a crowd,—cowboys, ranch girls, and a general horde of 'woollies.' Don't accuse her of it, Patty; get around her and see what she says."

"Goodness, Mona, give me credit for a little tact! I'll find out in the best way. What was the name of the play?"

"'Star of the West.' A splendid thing,—have you seen it?"

"No; we almost never go."

"Oh, we go a lot, we love moving pictures."

"I'd like to see this one,—before I speak to Azalea. Is it on now?"

"Yes, at The Campanile. Let's go down to-morrow,—just you

and me. We can be back in a couple of hours."

"Well, I'll see. Probably I can go."

In the meantime, Azalea and Van Reypen were talking of the same play.

"I saw a picture play last night," Phil was saying, "with a girl in it that looked exactly like you."

"What was the play?" asked Azalea, interestedly.

"'Star of the West.' It was a good play, but I was most interested in the girl I speak of. She was really your double, —but she did things that I don't believe you could compass, —athletic as you are."

"I'd like to see it," said Azalea, thoughtfully.

"Oh, go with me, will you? I'm going to stay up here over the week-end,—and we could skip down to-morrow afternoon, and be back by dinner time."

"I'd love to go,—but Patty doesn't greatly approve of the 'movies.'"

"Oh, never mind that. You've a right to go, if you choose. And you needn't say where we're going, till we get back. Say we're going to take in a matinee."

"Well, I'll go," Azalea said decidedly, "for I'm crazy to see that play. What's the girl's name?"

"Dunno. It wasn't on the bill. But, truly, Azalea, you'll be surprised to see how much like you she is!"

Azalea hesitated. She knew it was taking a great risk to go with Phil, but she was most anxious to see how she looked on the screen.

This, she knew, was the first picture released in which she had taken a part. It was only a small part, but she had done well, the manager said, and that had been the reason for her further advancement.

She had wanted to see it over at the studio, but her visits there had been so hurried, and she had been so eager to get back, she never dared take the time to see the pictures exhibited.

The two returned to the house, and Patty greeted them gaily.

"Well, wanderers, you're the last of the company to report! Where have you been?"

"Surveying your domain, ma'am," Phil replied; "it's most beautiful by moonlight,—especially when viewed in company with a fair lady."

He bowed gallantly to Azalea, who was looking her best,—a slight blush of excitement on her cheeks at the compliment.

"It *is* lovely," she said; "the house, from the west lawn, is a wonderful picture! Patty, Mr. Van Reypen has asked me to go to New York with him to-morrow afternoon,—to a matinee. May I?"

"Certainly, my child. And as Mona and I are going down in the early afternoon, we'll all go together in the big car."

Then all went to the hall for a dance. The large reception hall was admirably adapted for this purpose, and the strains of a fine phonograph soon set all feet in motion.

Dancing with Raymond Gale, Azalea pirouetted gaily with some fancy steps.

"Good!" he cried, falling into the spirit of the thing, and they pranced about in a mad whirl.

"How Western she is," Elise said to Phil, with whom she was sedately one-stepping.

"Clever dancer," he returned, briefly, and the subject was not continued.

"Come for a walk," said Gale to Azalea, as the dance was over.

"No; let's sit on the porch a minute," she preferred.

"Come along to this end, then, for I want to say something particular," he urged, and they found a pleasant seat, from which they could see the moon through the leafy wistaria branches.

"Look here, Azalea," Gale began, "I know what you're up to,—with the Bixbys."

"What!" Azalea's voice was full of fear.

"Yes, and there's no reason you should be so secretive about it."

"Oh, Raymond,—there *is* reason! Don't tell on me, will you?"

"Of course not,—if you forbid it. But when Farnsworth asks me, what am I to say?"

"What does he ask you?"

"Who the Bixbys are. And other awkward questions. You see, I know old Bixby,—and I knew as soon as I saw him here that day that he had drawn you into his snares."

"Don't put it that way—I wasn't exactly drawn in."

"Well, you're in, all right. Why, Azalea, I saw you in a picture in New York, night before last."

"You did?"

"Yes; in 'Star of the West.' Don't try to fib out of it—"

"What!"

"Now you needn't get mad! I know you're not entirely above a little fibbing, now and then!"

"I think I'll go in the house,—I don't like you."

"Oh, Zaly, behave yourself. Be a sensible girl, and face the music! Why don't you own it all up, and tell Farnsworth the whole story? It isn't a criminal thing to act in the 'movies.'"

"They think it is,—Bill and Patty. They'd never forgive me!"

"Oh, pshaw, they would, too! Anyway, I want you to do it, —tell 'em, I mean. Won't you, Zaly,—won't you,—for my sake?"

Gale was sincere and earnest, and Azalea thrilled to the strong tenderness in his voice as he urged her.

But she hesitated to consent.

"I can't, Ray," she said, at last. "Truly, I can't. They'd—they'd turn me off—"

"Oh, Azalea, what nonsense! They'd do no such thing!"

"Yes, they would. You don't know Bill. He's good and generous and kind,—but he hates anything like deceit,—and almost worse, he hates the whole moving-picture racket. I don't mean the pictures themselves, exactly,—but the idea of anybody of his being in them. And, oh, Ray,—it isn't only myself,—but I took—I took—"

"I know,—you took the kiddy."

"Yes, I did. It didn't seem any harm, at first, and then, one day when I brought her home,—she was sleepy,—unusually so, I mean, and Nurse said she had been given soothing sirup,—and—I found out afterward she had! Mrs. Bixby had given her some, to keep her quiet in the picture, you know. Of course, I never dreamed of such a thing,—why, Ray, that little girl is as dear to me,—almost,—as she is to Patty! I wouldn't harm a hair of her blessed little curly head! And I'd never have allowed a drop of that sirup, if I'd known it! But I just gave her to Mrs. Bixby to hold, while I changed my costume,—Mrs. Bixby seems a good woman—"

"Oh, come now, I don't believe it hurt the child."

"You don't know anything about such things. I don't know much, but I know they must never have a bit of that stuff! Anyway, Ray?—we must go in now,—don't give my secret away until I give you permission, will you?"

"No; if you'll promise to think it over and try to believe what I've told you,—that it's best to tell all."

"All right, I'll promise that, and I may decide to tell. But I want to wait until after to-morrow, anyway."

CHAPTER XIV

AT THE PICTURE PLAY

By a little adroit manoeuvring Van Reypen managed things so that he and Azalea did not go to New York in the motor with Patty and Mona, but went down by themselves in the train.

For Azalea was most anxious that Patty should not know she was going to the moving pictures, and especially that she was going to see "Star of the West."

It had already become a popular picture and was drawing crowds. And though Azalea's part in it was a small one, yet her work was so good that one or two reviews had mentioned it approvingly.

Azalea had hoped that it would be possible to let Van Reypen continue in his mistaken impression that the girl on the screen was not herself, but some one who looked marvellously like her.

But the first sight of herself in the play so thrilled Azalea that she was unable to repress an exclamation of surprised delight.

"It *is* you, Azalea!" whispered Phil, realising the truth. "How *did* you manage it? Oh, you wonderful girl!"

Azalea looked at him in astonishment. In the dim light of the theatre she could see his face glowing with pride and pleasure.

She gave a little gasp. "Oh, Phil, aren't you—I mean—are you *glad* about it?"

"I don't know,—Azalea,—it seems so queer—but, oh, look at that! Did you really do that, Azalea!"

For the girl on the screen had flung herself, bareback, on a vicious, bucking pony, and holding on by his mane, went through the most hairbreadth escapes, yet was not thrown. Indeed, she finally tamed the wild creature, and dashed madly off on her errand. This was the rescue of a baby who had been left behind, when those who should have looked after the child were themselves fleeing from a cyclone.

The scene was remarkably well staged, and the illusion of the cyclone wonderfully worked out.

The baby, left to the care of servants, was in a lightly built house that rocked in the blasts. It threatened to collapse at any minute, and Azalea, racing against time, in the face of the gale, spurred on her flying steed, and reached the house just as it crashed to ruins.

Flinging herself from the horse, she dashed into the piles of debris, and, the gale nearly blowing her off her feet, contrived to find the child.

Of course, in the taking of the picture, Fleurette had been in no danger whatever; in fact, had not been in the falling house at all, until time for Azalea to find her in the ruins.

But this was not apparent to the audience. To them it seemed that the baby must have been there all the time.

Van Reypen sat breathless, watching the screen with rapt attention.

He thought little of the baby's danger, knowing the methods of making pictures, but he was lost in admiration of Azalea, her fine athletic figure, and her free, strong motions, as she battled with the winds and triumphantly snatched the baby from harm.

Then, the child in one arm, she flung herself again on the pony's back, the animal prancing wildly, but tractable beneath Azalea's determined guidance, and they were off like the wind itself to a place of safety. The wild ride was picturesque, if frightful, and there was a burst of applause from the spectators, as Azalea, panting, exhausted, but safe, at last reached her goal, and leaning down from the horse, placed the baby in the arms of its weeping, distracted mother.

Azalea's beauty was of the sort that needs excitement or physical exertion to bring out its best effects and as she stood beside the quivering, spent horse, her own heart beating quickly, her own breath coming hard, she was a picture of vivid beauty.

Her dress was disordered, her hair hung in loosened coils, her collar was half torn off by the wind, but the happy smile and the justifiable pride in her success lighted up her countenance till it was fairly radiant.

"By cricky, you're stunning!" exclaimed Phil, under his breath, as he grasped her hand in congratulation.

And so, because of his praise and appreciation Azalea forgot her fears of censure from the Farnsworths and gave herself up to the delights of the moment.

She would not have felt so comfortable had she heard Patty's remarks at sight of the picture.

Patty and Mona had come to the theatre later than Azalea, and had been given seats on the other side of the large house. The darkness, too, made it unlikely that they should see each other, and so Azalea remained in blissful ignorance of Patty's presence.

* * * * *

"Of course, it's Azalea," Patty said to Mona, the moment the girl appeared on the screen. "I—oh, I don't know *what* to think about it,—but, isn't she splendid!"

"She is! That rig is most becoming to her, and she has such poise,—so strong and free, yet graceful."

"She's certainly at her best."

"Of course, the director saw her possibilities and has brought out all her best points. How pretty her hair is,—loose, like that."

"Yes, she's a real beauty,—of the true breezy, Western type. But, Mona, what *will* Bill say? I do believe I shall feel more lenient about it all than he will! He is conservative, you know, for all his Western bringing up. Oh, my gracious, Mona, *what's* she doing now?"

"She'll kill herself with that wild horse! She *never* can get on his back!"

In a state of great excitement, they watched Azalea's skilful management of the pony and clutched each other's hands in speechless fear as she tore through the gale to rescue her brother's child.

And then—when at last Azalea emerged from the tumbled-down ruin of the little old house, with a baby in her arms, Patty gave a cry of startled fear, and then clapped her hand over her mouth, lest her dismay be too evident to those sitting near by.

"Mona!" she whispered, "it's Fleurette!"

"No! I don't believe it! You can't tell,—such a *little* baby—they all look alike,—you're imagining, Patty—"

"It is! it *is*! That's where they went when Azalea took Baby off for a whole day,—and two or three times for an afternoon or a morning! Oh, I can't *stand* it!"

Patty buried her face in her hands and refused to look up while Azalea rode the galloping horse, with the child held fast in one arm.

Mona felt it must be true. To be sure she couldn't really recognise Fleurette's face, but she was certain that Patty's mother heart could make no mistake, and it was small wonder that she was overcome at seeing her child in such scenes.

"Hush, Patty," said Mona, as Patty's sobs began to sound hysterical, "hush,—this is only a picture, you know,—this isn't really Fleurette,—she is safe at home—"

"But she must have been here! Azalea *must* have carried her, *really*—on that terrific horse! They couldn't have got the pictures if she hadn't!"

"Well, it's all right, anyway. It didn't hurt the baby—"

"Oh, hush, Mona! you don't know what I'm suffering! I guess if your baby had been taken off and put through such awful doings, you'd know what I feel! My baby,—my little flower baby! In that awful crashing, tumbling down old shanty! Oh, I *can't* stand it!"

"Let's go out, Patty, there's no reason for us to stay longer."

"Yes, let's," and gathering up her wraps, Patty rose to go.

They made their way out of the dark, crowded place, and finding the motor-car, they went straight home.

Once there, Patty flew to the nursery, and fairly snatching the baby from Nurse Winnie's arms, she held it close, and crooned loving little broken songs.

"You're all right," Mona said, laughing at her. "You've got your baby, safe and sound,—now just sit down there and enjoy her for a while."

This Patty gladly did, and Mona went in search of Farnsworth.

She finally found him, down in a distant garden, where he was looking after some planting matters.

"Come along o' me," she said, smiling at him.

Wonderingly Farnsworth looked up.

"Thought you girls went to the city," he said.

"We did,—also, we returned. Patty is in the nursery, and I want a few minutes' talk with you."

"O.K.," and the big man gave some parting instructions to a gardener and then went off with Mona. She led him to a nearby arbour, and commenced at once.

"You and I are old friends," she said, "and so I'm going to take an old friend's privilege and give you some advice, and also ask a few questions. First, who is Azalea?"

"My two or three times removed cousin."

"Are you sure?"

Farnsworth looked at her. "What do you mean, Mona?"

"What I say; are you *sure?*"

"Funny thing to ask. Well,—I am and—I'm not."

"Now, what do *you* mean?"

"I'll tell you." And then he told her how queer he thought it that Azalea had had no letters from her father since her arrival,—nor any letters at all from Horner's Corners.

"And she's so sly about it," he wound up; "why once she wrote a letter to herself, and pretended it was from her father!"

"I can't make it out," Mona mused. "If her father were dead, she'd have no reason to conceal the fact. Nor if he had remarried. And if he has done anything disgraceful—maybe that's it, Bill! Maybe he's in jail!"

"I've thought of that, Mona, and, of course, it's a possibility. That would explain her not getting letters, and her unwillingness to tell the reason. But,—somehow, it isn't very plausible. Why shouldn't she confide in me? I've begged her to,—and no matter what Uncle Thorpe may have done, it's no real reflection on Azalea."

"No; but now *I've* something to tell you about the girl."

Mona gave him a full account of the moving-picture play that she and Patty had visited, and told him, too, of Patty's distress over the pictures of Fleurette.

Farnsworth was greatly amazed, but, like Mona, he knew Patty could not be mistaken as to the identity of Fleurette.

"And I just thought," Mona went on, "that I'd tell you before Patty did,—for,—oh, well, this is my real reason,—Patty is so wrought up and so wild over the Fleurette matter that she can't judge Azalea fairly,—and I don't want to have injustice done to her at this stage of the game. For, Bill, Azalea has real talent,—real dramatic genius, *I* think, and if there's no reason against it,—except conventional ones,—I think she ought to be allowed to become a motion-picture actress. She's bound to make good,—she has the right sort of a face for the screen,—beautiful, mobile, expressive, and really, a speaking countenance. Why, she'd make fame and fortune, I'm positive."

"Oh, Mona! what utter rubbish! One of *our* people in the 'movies'! Impossible!"

"I knew you'd say that! And I know Patty will say—oh, good Heavens, I don't know *what* Patty will say! But I do know this; she would have been sensible and would have felt just as I do about it, if it hadn't been for the Fleurette part of it. Before the baby appeared on the screen Patty was really delighted with Azalea. She was enthusiastic about her talent and her beauty,— really, Bill, she looked very beautiful in the pictures."

"Oh, Zaly is good-looking enough. But her taking our baby is—why, there's no term suitable! Where is Azalea!"

"I hope nowhere near, while you look like that!" and Mona laughed. "Your expression is positively murderous!"

"I feel almost that way! Just think, Mona, Azalea is *my* relative! I inflicted her on Patty, poor little Patty—"

"Oh, come now, Bill, don't overdo it! Azalea was most daring and even foolish, but not criminal. You know how she loves that child, and you know she wouldn't let harm come near her."

"But accidents might happen, for all Azalea's care and watchfulness—"

"I know that, but an accident might happen to Winnie when she takes Baby out in her coach!"

"Are you standing up for Azalea?"

"That's just what I'm doing! I'm glad you've got it through your head at last. And I ask this of you, old friend. Whatever you do or say to Azalea, think it well over beforehand. If you talk to Patty, as she is feeling now you'll both be ready to tar and feather poor Zaly; and, truly, she doesn't deserve it! Please, Bill, go slow,—and be just. Be generous if you can,—but at any rate, be just. That's all I ask. And you can't be just if you act on impulse,—so, go slow. Will you?"

"Yes, Mona,—there's my hand on it We're not often over-impulsive,—Patty and I,—but in this case we may be,—might have been,—if you hadn't warned me. You're a good girl, Mona, and I thank you for your foresight and real kindness,"

And so Farnsworth went in search of Patty with a resolve to try to reason out the matter with a fair consideration of all sides of it.

He found his wife and daughter in the nursery.

Patty had sent Winnie off, feeling that she must hold Fleurette in her arms for some time, in order to realise that she was safe from the whirling winds of that awful cyclone!

When Bill appeared, Patty began at once, and launched forth a full description of the picture play, and of Azalea's and Fleurette's parts in it.

Farnsworth sat looking at her, his blue eyes full of a contented admiration. To this simple-minded, big-hearted man, his wife and child represented the whole world. All he had, all he owned, he valued only for the pleasure it might mean to them.

"Darling," he said, as she finished the tale, "what do *you* think about it all?"

"Mona's been talking to you!" Patty cried, with sudden intuition.

"What! How do you know? You clair-voyant!"

"Of course I know," and Patty wagged a wise head at him. "First, because you're not sufficiently surprised,—she told you all about it! And second, because you're not furious at Azalea! Mona has talked you around to her way of thinking,—which is, that Azalea is a genius,—and that—"

"That Fleurette is another! Think of being on the screen at the tender age of six months!"

"You're a wretch! you're a monster! you're a—a—dromedary!"

Patty was feeling decidedly better about the whole matter. Having sat for nearly an hour, holding and fondling her idolised child, she realised that whatever Fleurette had gone through, she was safe now,—and that whatever was to be done to Azalea by way of punishment, was more Bill's affair than hers.

"You don't care two cents for your wonder-child! Your own little buttercup,—your daffy-downdilly baby!" she cried, in pretended reproof, and then Farnsworth took Fleurette and tossed her about until she squealed with glee.

"Oh, I guess we'll keep her," he said, as he handed her back to her mother's arms. "She's the paragon baby of the whole world, even if I don't appreciate her."

"Oh, you do! you *do*!" exclaimed Patty, remorseful now at having teased him. "And now, Sweet William, what's *your* idea of a right and proper punishment for Cousin Azalea?"

"That's a matter for some thought," he responded, mindful of Mona's words. "Look here, Patty, quite aside from Fleurette's connection with this case,—what's your opinion of Zaly as a 'movie' star?"

"She's great, dear,—she really is. And—if she weren't our relative—"

"*My* relative—"

"*Our* relative, I should advise her to go in for the thing seriously; but,—I may be over-conservative,—even snobbish, but I do hate to have our cousin's portrait all over the fences and ashbarrels, and in all the Sunday papers, and—"

"I don't mind that publicity so much as I do the possible effects on Azalea's life. I don't know that the career of a 'movie' star is as full of dangerous pitfalls as the theatrical line, but—I hate to see Azalea subjected to them,—for her own sake."

"I'm not sure we'll have anything to say in the matter," Patty observed, thoughtfully.

"She may take the bit in her own teeth. After seeing her break that bucking broncho to-day,—I don't think her as tractable and easily influenced as I did!"

"How's this plan, dearest? Suppose we don't tell Azalea, for the moment, that you saw the picture to-day, and see what she'll do next."

"All right, I'd be glad to think it over a little. We'll warn Mona not to give it away,—and nobody else knows we went there."

"Of course, I'll take up the matter of Fleurette with Azalea, separately," Farnsworth went on. "But even if she's determined on her career, I feel sure we can persuade her to leave her little assistant out of it!"

"I rather just guess we can!" and Patty cuddled the baby to her breast. "Well, the crowd will gather on the porch soon. I'll make a fresh toilette and play the serene hostess, once again."

Fleurette was given over to Winnie, and Patty, calm and happy now, ran off to dress.

Carolyn Wells

"You're such a darling,—Big Billee," she whispered turning back to her husband, and she went into his embracing arms; "you always know just what is right to do."

"Especially when Mona coaches me beforehand," he laughed, unwilling to deceive her in the slightest degree.

"Pooh," said Patty, "you're so right, even Mona can't make you any righter!"

CHAPTER XV

SOME RECORDS

"Sur le pont
D'Avignon,
On y dansait, on y dansait,
Sur le pont
D'Avignon,
On y dansait tout le rond!"

Patty's sweet, clear soprano notes rang out gaily as she trilled the little song she had picked up in France.

"What a pretty thing," cried Elise, "teach it to me, do, Patty."

"All right, I will. But there's a record of it,—my singing,—for the phonograph. You'll learn it better from that."

"All right; Chick, come and find the record for me."

The two went into the library, leaving the others on the porch.

It was Sunday afternoon, and everybody was idle and happy. Patty was a good hostess and did not bother her guests by over-entertaining them.

But at Wistaria Porch there was always enough to do, if any one wanted to do it,—and delightful lounging places, if one were indolently inclined.

Searching among the catalogued records, Chick easily found the one Elise wanted.

"What a lot of records they have of the baby's voice!" he exclaimed.

"Yes," Elise assented, "they make them on all occasions. Patty's keeping them for her, when she grows up. Clever idea."

"Yes, but she'll have to build a town hall to keep them in! The child hasn't begun to talk yet, but here are dozens—"

"Oh, well, they'll weed them out. Some of them are awful cunning,—and one is a first-class crying spell! They never could get but one of Fleurette crying, she's such a good-natured kiddy. All right, Chick,—start it off."

They listened to the pretty little *chanson*, and repeated it until Elise felt satisfied she had added it to her repertory.

Just as she finished Betty Gale came flying in.

"Skip into your togs, Elise, and come for a drive with us," she said. "I've corralled Bill and Patty,—and Ray wants you,—and I," she looked saucily at Channing, "I want Mr. Chick."

"We're with you to the last ditch!" Channing replied and Elise went off for her hat.

"Shall I put away these records?" Chick asked looking at several they had been using.

"No," said Betty, carelessly, "Patty has hordes of minions who do such things. Leave them, and get your duster on. We're off,—*pronto!*"

"Where's Azalea?" Raymond Gale inquired, as, a few moments later, he had his merry party in his car, and took hold of the wheel.

"She and Van Reypen went for a long walk," Farnsworth replied. "And the married Farringtons have gone back to town, so this is all our party—for the moment."

"All right; here we go, then." And the big car rolled down the driveway.

"I hesitated about going," Patty demurred, "for it's Winnie's Sunday out, and I had to leave baby with Janet. I've never done it before."

"Oh, well," Betty laughed, "she'll probably sleep till you get back. Don't babies always sleep all the afternoon?"

"Not always, but Fleurette often does. Oh, of course, she'll be all right"

"And Azalea isn't there," she added, in a low tone to her husband.

And indeed, just then, Azalea was far away from there.

She and Phil had gone for the sort of walk they both loved,— along woodland paths, cross-lots, now and then back on the highroad, and if they got too far to walk back, prepared to return by train or trolley.

The two were congenial spirits, which fact had rather surprised Van Reypen's friends. For he was a conservative, fastidious aristocrat, and though Azalea's rough edges had been rubbed down a bit by Patty's training, she was still of a very different type from the Van Reypen stock.

But they both loved the open, and they strode along, chatting or silent as fitted their mood.

"What's in your mind just now, Brownie?" he asked, as Azalea looked thoughtful.

"Why,—a queer sort of a notion. Did you ever have a premo-nition,—a sort of feeling that you ought to do something—"

"A hunch?"

"Yes; a presentiment that unless you do what you're told to do, there'll be trouble—"

"Who told you?"

"That's just it. Nobody,—except a—oh, a mysterious force, a—just an impulse, you know."

"Obey it if you like. May I go, too?"

"Well, it's this. Just before we turned that last corner a motor passed us, you know."

"Yes, I saw it. One of Farnsworth's,—with some of the servants in it."

"It was. Patty gives them rides in turn. Now, Winnie the nurse was in, and so it must be her Sunday out. And, of course, Patty is home there with the baby,—she never leaves her if Winnie's away, but still—I feel as if I must go home to look after that child!"

"Is that all? Let's go, then. We can walk back as well as to go on."

"But,—don't laugh, now,—I feel we ought to hurry. Let's take the trolley-car,—it isn't far to the line."

"You sure have got a hunch! But your will is my law. Wish we were near a garage,—I'm not a bit fond of Sunday trolley riding!"

"I'm not either,—but, Phil, you're awful good not to laugh at me."

"Bless your soul, I've no notion of laughing at you! Your presentiment may be the real thing,—for all I know. Anyway, if you want to go home, you're going."

So go they did, and, by the trolley-car route, arrived at the house in half an hour.

As they passed the Gales' place, on their way from the car-line to the house, Van Reypen said, "Guess I'll stop here a minute if you don't mind. I left my pet pipe here yesterday. Skip along home, and I'll follow."

Azalea went on and was surprised to find the house deserted.

She went straight to the nursery, and found Fleurette in the care of Janet, who was substitute nurse in Winnie's absence.

"Everything all right, Janet?" said Azalea.

"Yes, Miss Thorpe. Baby's had her milk, and I think she'll soon go to sleep."

"She doesn't look much like it now," and Azalea smiled at the gurgling, laughing child, who was wide awake and in frolicsome mood.

"Where's Mrs. Farnsworth?" Azalea asked.

"She went motoring with Miss Gale. They all went,—and all the help have gone too. I'm alone in the house with the baby."

"Glad I came home, then. Mr. Van Reypen is here too, and I think I'll take Fleurette down on the porch for half an hour. When she gets sleepy I'll bring her up here."

"Very well, Miss Thorpe. I'll be here."

Janet busied herself about the nursery and Azalea went downstairs with the baby in her arms.

On the vine-shaded porch they sat, and as Van Reypen stayed chatting with some of the Gale family, Azalea and the baby were each other's sole companions.

Their conversation was a little one-sided, but Azalea's remarks were mostly eulogies and compliments and Fleurette's engaging smiles seemed to betoken appreciation if not acknowledgment.

A footstep approaching made Azalea look up.

Before her stood Mr. Merritt, the assistant director of the film company.

"Good afternoon, Miss Thorpe," he said, politely; "I see the little one is in a sunshiny mood."

"Yes;" Azalea returned, but her very soul quaked with fear. Well she knew what was in this man's mind.

"And so, I'm going to ask you to run over to the studio just a few minutes and give us one more chance at a good picture of that scene."

"And I'm going to refuse," Azalea returned with spirit. "You know very well, Mr. Merritt, that I'm not going to let you pose this child again."

"I know you *are*,—and mighty quick, too," he retorted, in a low voice, but tones of great determination. "I know everybody is out,—you are practically alone in the house, and I know you're coming with me,—willing or not! It won't hurt the baby a mite,—I've my little car out in the road,—and if you *don't* consent,—I'll—"

He voiced no threat, but Azalea felt pretty sure he meant to take the baby himself if she refused to go with them.

She thought quickly, but no avenue of escape could she see. It would be utterly useless to call Janet, for she was a nervous, timid girl, and would probably run away at sight of this strange man.

The nursery, too, was on the other side of the house, and she couldn't make Janet hear if she tried.

The Gale house also was on the other side of the Farnsworth house, and so, indeed, if Azalea chose to call for help, it would do no good. Doubtless Phil would be along shortly, but there was no telling, for there was always a merry crowd on the Gale's piazza and he would stay there talking for a time.

But Merritt was impatient, and he finally broke out with; "Make up your mind, please, and quickly. Will you bring the baby quietly, or shall I just—take her along."

He held out his arms to Fleurette, who, always ready to make friends with strangers, smiled and leaned toward him.

Azalea had wild thoughts of running away,—anywhere,—but she knew the futility of such a plan. Merritt was a big and strong man, and though Azalea was a swift runner, she could not get a start without his intervening.

She tried pleading. She appealed to his manliness, his kindness, his generosity,—all with no success.

"Don't talk rubbish," he said, shortly; "you know as well as I do, it won't hurt the child. In fact, I came to get her to-day, myself, because I knew her nurse was out,—and I saw you go off,—and later, all the rest of the bunch. If *you* hadn't come back,—confound you! I'd have had that child over there by this time!"

Azalea gasped. So her premonition had been a true one after all! Had she not returned, Merritt would have easily overcome Janet and taken the baby off with him. She knew they would not harm Fleurette,—indeed, would be most careful of her.

Unless, perhaps, they should give her soothing-sirup again. Well they'd get no chance, for Azalea was determined the baby should not be taken from her, and she most certainly was not going herself.

"You know what it will mean to you," Merritt threatened; "if I so advise Bixby, he'll throw you over. How'd you like to lose your job now that you've just begun to make good?"

"That's nothing to do with it," Azalea said, trying to speak calmly and not show how frightened she was.

But Merritt discerned it.

"All right," he said, "sorry you won't listen to reason,—but since you won't,—guess I'll have to use force."

He took hold of Fleurette's little arm, to lift her from Azalea's lap, and the touch roused the girl's wrath to boiling point.

"Don't you dare!" she cried, holding the baby tightly. "Leave, —leave at once! or I'll call for help!"

She rose, as if to make good her threat, though she knew there was no help within call.

Merritt knew it too, and he laughed at her.

"Stop this nonsense, now," he commanded roughly. "I'm going to accomplish what I came here for, so you may as well take it quietly. I can take the child without a whimper from her,—and you know it! So, why not be sensible and come along too, and look out for her yourself?"

"You shall not take her!" Azalea looked like an angry tigress.

"Gee! Wish I had you on the screen like that! You're some picture!"

"Please, Mr. Merritt," Azalea tried coaxing again, "please believe me,—I can't take Fleurette again. Her mother—why, Mr. Merritt, you have children of your own—"

"Sure I have! That's how I know how to treat 'em so well. If mine were only small enough, I wouldn't need this little cutie. Well, here goes, then!"

This time he laid such a definite hold on the baby, that Azalea could scarcely keep the child in her own arms.

In her utter desperation, a new idea struck her. She would try strategy.

"Oh, don't!" she cried, "rather than have you touch her, I'll go—I'll take her. Let me get her cap and coat."

"Where are they?" he asked, suspiciously.

"Right here, in the library,—just across the hall."

"Go on, then,—I trust you, 'cause I think you're sensible. I'd go along and keep you in sight, but I want to keep watch if anybody comes. But you sing, or whistle or something, so's I'll know you're right there."

"All right," and Azalea's heart beat fast, for she had a splendid scheme.

Into the library she carried Fleurette, singing as she went, and once in the room, she put the baby on a chair and flew for the record rack.

Quickly she found the record of the baby's crying spell and put it in place in the phonograph.

Then, picking up Fleurette, she set the needle going and hurried from the room.

Merritt, hearing the cries, screams and sobs, scowled with anger at the baby's fit of ill temper, but never dreamed that it was not really the child crying at all.

So Azalea had ample chance to escape by a back door from the library, and crossing the dining-room went out on a side porch that faced the Gale place.

Looking carefully to see that Merritt had not followed her, and listening a moment to learn how much longer the record,—of which she knew every familiar sound,—would last, she ran with all the speed of which she was capable over to the Gales'.

Van Reypen was just taking leave, and he, as well as the others present, looked in amazement at the flying figure coming nearer and nearer until Azalea reached the group.

"Take her," she said to Mrs. Gale, as she gave her the baby, "keep her safe—*safe*!"

And then Azalea went flying back.

The record was finished,—and with the sudden stop of the child's crying Merritt had started into the library to see what it meant.

There Azalea found him, and she faced him bravely.

"That baby is safe," she said, "where you can't get at her! And now I will tell you what I think of *you*! You are a thief and a scoundrel! You don't deserve to be allowed to carry on a reputable business! I don't want any further connection with you or your company. I am proud to be fired from such a lot of bandits as you people are!"

So angry was she, and so unguarded as to what she was saying that she fairly flung the words at him.

For a moment he was stunned at her wild tirade, and then his artist instinct was stirred,—for the picture she made was beautiful and dramatic. She had no thought of this, for she was in earnest, and her whole soul was up in arms at thought of the threatened abduction of Fleurette. And, so, knowing that the child was safe with Mrs. Gale, she let the vials of her wrath pour forth on the villain who had so aroused it, and her voice was raised in scathing obloquy.

"All right!" Merritt said, as she paused from sheer want of breath, "I'll take my beating, if you'll go over to the studio with me and repeat this scene. Let me pose you while you're in this humour,—you'll never reach such heights again!"

"Nor will I ever pose for you again! I'm through with you,—all of you, and all the moving-picture business! I was warned to keep out of it,—but I didn't know what wretches I would find in it! Go! Go at once! and never let me see your face again!"

It was at this moment that the Gale motor party returned.

Patty and Bill, hearing Azalea's loud tones, rushed to the library and found her there with Merritt.

"Where's Baby?" Patty cried, starting for the stairs.

"She's safe, Patty," Azalea said, stopping her. "She's all right, —she's over to Mrs. Gale's."

"Mrs. Gale's!" and Patty flew off like the wind, caring for nothing but the assurance of her own eyes that Fleurette was safe.

"Help me, Bill," said Azalea, going toward Farnsworth, "you said once, you'd defend me."

"I will, dear. What's this all about? Who are *you*?" He addressed Merritt quietly, but with a fire in his blue eyes that was disturbing.

"Merritt, of the Flicker Film Company, very much at your service," and the man drew a card from his pocket and presented it.

"Well, Mr. Merritt, leave at once, and never return. I don't care for your explanations or excuses. Simply *go*."

Merritt went.

"Is that right, Zaly?" Bill said, as the crestfallen visitor left them. "I didn't want any words with him,—for I might have lost my temper. I'd rather have the story from you."

"And I'll tell it to you,—all. But, oh, Bill, I'm so *glad* Fleurette is all right!"

"She is *so*!" and Patty came dancing on, with the smilingest child in the world. Van Reypen followed, and then the whole crowd drew together anxious to know what the commotion was all about.

CHAPTER XVI

AZALEA'S STORY

"Yes, I'll tell you the whole story," Azalea repeated, addressing herself to Farnsworth, but glancing now and then at the others.

"On my way East, I met Mr. and Mrs. Bixby on the train. They were pleasant people and Mrs. Bixby was very kind to me in many ways. Then, I learned that they were in the moving-picture business, and as I wanted to act myself, I cultivated their acquaintance all I could. And by the time we reached New York Mr. Bixby had agreed to give me a trial at his studio. He said I had the right type of face for the screen and if I could learn to act, my Western life had fitted me for some certain parts they were just then in need of. So I went in for it,—and I got along all right. Then they wanted a little baby in the picture and as I was so fond of Fleurette and loved her too much to let any harm come to her, I thought it all right to take her over there once or twice to get the pictures of her. But one of the films went wrong, somehow, and Mr. Merritt was determined to take it over again. I wouldn't allow it, because I found out how Patty felt about Baby being in it,—so I refused. Now, I don't suppose you know how insistent the picture people are about any scene they want. They go to any lengths to get them. I've heard Mr. Bixby say, 'Get the picture if it kills the leading man!' And though he doesn't mean that literally I think he would do anything short of murder to get his picture. Well, they thought that the whole reel was spoiled because one scene with Fleurette in it wasn't right. And they were bound to have her over there again."

"She shan't go,—so she shouldn't!" Patty crooned, as she held her child closer in her sheltering arms.

"No; and that's what I told Mr. Merritt," went on Azalea. "But he is tricky, and I felt pretty sure he'd try underhand means to get the baby. I've kept watch night and day, and I've always been certain that Fleurette was either in Winnie's care or Patty's. Patty wouldn't trust her with *me* any more."

Azalea spoke the last words wistfully, with a penitent look in her brown eyes.

"Small wonder!" cried Elise, who was listening interestedly. "After you took that blessed child to—"

"There, there, Elise," Farnsworth interrupted, "we *do* trust Azalea. Let her finish her story."

Azalea gave him a grateful look and went on.

"When I went away from the house to-day, Patty was at home, so, though I knew it was Winnie's day off, I felt all right about Baby. Then,—while we were out walking, I saw Winnie go by,—and soon after I felt a—a sort of presentiment that I *must* go home. I couldn't tell why,—only I felt I must come back to the house at once. So I did,—and everything seemed to be all right. I decided I had been foolishly nervous about it,—and I took Fleurette down on the porch for a little while.

"Then that man came and demanded her! I was alone, except for Janet,—who is no good in an emergency,—and Mr. Merritt was very determined. If I hadn't thought of the phonograph I don't know what I should have done, for that man is quite capable of taking Baby away from my arms by main force. But I happened to think I could fool him,—as I couldn't combat him,—so I put on the crying record to make him think we were still in the library,—and I scooted over to Gales' with the baby as fast as I could run. Then I came back—"

"Weren't you afraid of him?" asked Patty, shuddering at the thought of Azalea at the mercy of the infuriated man.

"No; I know him, and he isn't a brute or a ruffian. He was just bent on getting Fleurette for that picture,—it would take only a few minutes,—and I was just as bent that he shouldn't.

"So, when he found I had outwitted him, he accepted the situation,—why, he even wanted to take *my* picture in my angry mood! He is a man who thinks of nothing but a good pose for his pictures."

"He seemed a decent chap," Farnsworth said, "but I was so angry, I just fired him, for I feared otherwise I'd lose control of my own temper and give him his just deserts!"

"He'll never come again," observed Van Reypen, "I saw you, Bill, when you invited him to leave! I'm no craven, but I shouldn't care to return to any one who had looked at me like that!"

"I *was* a bit positive," laughed Farnsworth. "But, Azalea, I must admit I'm rather bowled over by this idea of you in the moving pictures! It—it isn't done much in our crowd, you know."

"I know it,—and I'm never going to do it again! I've had enough! I wanted to make it my career,—but," she hesitated, "that was before I knew you—you nice people. I—I never knew *really* nice people before,—my Western friends are—are different. But I want to be like you," her troubled glance took in Patty and Bill and then drifted to the others; and her face was wistful and only lighted up as she looked at Van Reypen. He smiled encouragingly at her, and she continued.

"I'm quite ready to give up all connection with the Bixby people and I'll promise never to go near them again,—even if they try to get me to."

"You bet you won't!" exclaimed Farnsworth. "I'm glad you've given it up of your own accord, Zaly, for if you hadn't I'd have to forbid it, anyway! I can't allow you to do such things."

"And I don't want to. It wasn't as nice as I thought it would be, and yet,—it *was* fun!" She smiled as thoughts of her daredevil stunts passed through her mind.

"Tell us all about it!" cried Ray Gale. "I'm awfully interested, and *I'm* sorry you're going to quit! By George, Farnsworth! if you'd seen our Azalea in that picture of the cyclone!"

"Never mind!" Azalea interrupted him, "I'm all over that foolish idea."

"I should hope so!" exclaimed Elise, with a withering glance. "The idea of anybody being in such company as you must have been—"

"Not at all," Azalea declared; "I wasn't mixed up with anybody unpleasant at all. In fact, I talked to no one but the Bixbys and Mr. Merritt. Mrs. Bixby was most kind and looked after me as a mother might have done,—though I never knew a mother's care."

The pretty face grew sad, and the whole attitude of Azalea was so penitent and full of resolve to be more like the people she admired that all of Patty's lingering resentment fled away. She put the baby in her father's arms, and she flew over to Azalea and gave her an embrace of full and free forgiveness and affection.

"It's all right, Zaly," she said, smiling at her, "you *did* cut up jinks with my baby,—but when you came home to look after her,—even when you thought I was here,—and when you put up such a great game to rescue her from the enemy's clutches, —and succeeded,—well,—*I'm* for *you!*"

Patty spoke so whole-heartedly there was no doubt of her sincerity, and Azalea looked grateful and pleased,—yet, she looked troubled too.

"Oh, Patty, you're too good to me," she said, "you don't know —I don't deserve your faith and loyalty."

"Oh, I 'spect you do," and Patty caressed the shining brown hair.

"No,—I'm all unworthy—"

"I suppose you mean about that sampler business," put in Elise, with an unkind look on her face. "I think you ought to confess that,—while you're confessing."

Farnsworth gave a reproving glance at Elise, but he said, "Out with it, Zaly,—let's clean off the slate while we're about it. What's the sampler business that sticks in Elise's throat?"

He sounded so sympathetic and helpful that Azalea spoke up bravely.

"I did do wrong, Bill, but I didn't realise *how* wrong when I was doing it. I had an old sampler and it was dated 1836 and I picked out some stitches so it looked like 1636."

"You didn't deceive anybody!" exclaimed Elise.

"I'm glad of it," returned Azalea, simply. "I was too ignorant to know that there were no samplers made at that earlier date, —and to tell the truth, I didn't think much about it,—I just did it hastily,—on a sudden impulse,—because I wanted to give Elise something worth-while for her booth at the fair."

"And gave me something utterly worthless!" scoffed Elise.

"Oh, come now, Elise," said Farnsworth, "it didn't hurt your sales any, even if it didn't help them. Call it a joke and let it go at that."

"But it *was* deceitful, Cousin William," said Azalea, "and I do confess it, and I'm sorry as I can be about it."

Her pretty face was troubled and she looked so disturbed that Phil took up the cudgels for her.

"Oh, come off, all of you," he said, laughingly, "this isn't a court of inquiry, and we're not sitting in judgment on Azalea. She has properly admitted all her escapades, and she's been forgiven by the ones most interested, now let's call it a day, —and talk about something else."

"All right,—let's talk about the 'Star of the West,'" cried the irrepressible Ray Gale. "Now the secret's out, there's no harm in mentioning it. You *must* see that picture, Farnsworth, and then you'll be begging Azalea to go back to screen work!"

"Never," said Azalea, her face shining with happiness that she was forgiven and reinstated in general favour, "I've had my lesson. No more films for me! From now on, I'm going to be goody-girl,—and behave like nice ladies,—like Patty and Betty—and Elise."

The slight hesitation before the last name made Elise bite her lip in chagrin, for she had seen that her attack on Azalea was not approved of by most of the audience.

Poor Elise was of an unfortunate disposition, and envy and jealousy were her besetting sins. She had never liked Azalea for the reason that the Western girl, with her frank, untutored ways, often usurped Elise's place in the limelight, and Miss Farrington greatly objected to that.

It was with malicious purpose that Elise had brought up the subject of the sampler, and when she found it passed over as of little moment, she was angry at herself for having raised the question at all.

"Don't try to be like me," she said, with an acid smile at Azalea; "if you do, *nobody* will like you."

"Oh, come, now, Elise," said Farnsworth, laughing at this tempest in a teapot, "play fair. We all like you, and we all like Azalea, whether she models herself on you or not; so let's all love one another,—and let it go at that!"

"Yes," said Patty, "and now, my fellow lovers and loveresses, I must take my small daughter in and send her to sleepy-by, and the rest of you have just about half an hour before it's time to dress for dinner. The two Gales may consider themselves invited,—if they will honour us."

"Delighted," replied Betty, "though not overwhelmingly surprised at the invitation. Howsumever, we must fly back home for some purple and fine linen, and then we'll return anon. I'm usually returning here, anon! I wonder what I ever did, Patty, before you came here to live as our hospitable neighbours!"

"There's half an hour, Azalea," said Van Reypen, "come for a toddle down to the brook, and let's talk things over."

The two started off, and for a few moments walked along in silence.

Azalea was in a quiet, chastened mood,—a side of her character that Phil had never before seen, and he noted with pleasure the gentle sweetness of her face and the soft tones of her voice.

"It woke me up," she said, reminiscently, "when that man tried to take Fleurette from my arms. I would have fought him like a tiger if I hadn't suddenly realised that the way to fix *him* was by strategy. I just happened to think that by means of the record I could fool him into believing we were in the library, when really we were flying to refuge. I knew he wouldn't come in as long as he felt sure we were there, for he was watching out for the Farnsworths' return. So, I tried the scheme, and it worked!"

"Then you went bravely back to face the music!"

"Oh, I wasn't afraid of him,—for myself. He's not at all a ruffian sort,—and he never would have hurt the baby. Only, —he was bound to get her!"

"Well, he didn't succeed,—thanks to you, and I don't think he'll ever try it again."

"Oh, I'm sure he won't! He's afraid of Bill, all right! Any one would be who had seen the gleam in Cousin William's eyes when he fired Mr. Merritt!"

Azalea laughed a little at the recollection,—then she sighed.

"Why the sigh?" asked Van Reypen, looking at the expressive face of the girl, as her smile faded and her sensitive mouth drooped at the corners.

"Oh,—nothing—and everything! Don't ask questions!" She shook her shoulders as if flinging off a troublesome thought. "I want to forget the whole subject,—let's talk of other things."

"All right,—let's. Let's talk of my unworthy self, for instance."

"Why do you say your 'unworthy self'? Because you so look on yourself? or for the sake of being contradicted? or just for nonsense?"

The brown eyes smiled into his, and Azalea looked very roguish and saucy as she demanded an answer.

"Habit, I daresay. It's considered the thing for one to look upon himself as unworthy. Of course, I'm not all to the bad!"

"No, I suppose not. I've noticed saving graces now and then."

"You have! What, for instance? You see, I love to talk about myself!"

"Well, for one thing, you've been very kind to me. I was in a sorry position to-day, and you and Cousin William backed me up so beautifully, that I pulled through. If you hadn't I'd have collapsed and given up the game, in sheer fright."

"What do you mean?"

"Yes; Patty was pretty hostile at first,—though she came round all right, later. Elise was,—oh, well, you know Elise's attitude toward me."

"Don't mind her,—she's always got a chip on her shoulder!"

"Betty was reserving decision, too; and but for the strong support of you and Cousin William,—yes, and Ray Gale,—I shouldn't have come off so well. But I deserved any fate. I *have* been bad,—and though I am sorry,—that doesn't wipe it all out."

"It does, as far as I'm concerned. And I'm all that matters—at least,—I wish I might be all that matters."

"My gracious! There are lots who matter more than you! Patty and Bill, and Fleurette and—"

"Stop there! That's all! I'll concede those,—but no others. Don't you dare say that Gale matters more than I do!"

"Ray Gale? Oh, I don't know. And what do you mean by 'matters'?"

"Counts. Makes a difference. Affects you. Means something

to you."

"Oh, hold on! I'm floundering beyond my depth! Help! help!"

Azalea put her hands over her ears and shook her head, laughing at Van Reypen's earnest face as he racked his brain for further explanatory phrases.

"I won't stop! I'm in earnest. I *want* to matter—to mean something to you! I want to count with you—"

"Kipling says, 'let all men count with you, and none too much.'"

"Well, I'd rather count too much than not at all. Oh, Azalea,—you do understand me, don't you? Let me count, dear,—let me count for everything in your life—"

Azalea Thorpe couldn't believe her ears. What Van Reypen was saying seemed as if it could have but one meaning,—yet that was impossible! Philip Van Reypen, the high-born, aristocratic Philip, couldn't be seriously interested in a crude, ignorant Western girl!

"Thank you, Phil," she said, resolving to accept his words as a sign of friendship, "you're awfully good to me, and your friendship counts. I begin to think friendship is the one thing in life that does count. And it is the friends I have made—lately,—here,—that have made me see,—made me realise my own unworthiness,—and when I say that, I mean it."

"I won't let you mean it!" he cried, "I won't let you call yourself unworthy. For you count with me,—Azalea, more than the whole world! More than anything or everything in the world. Can't I count that way with you,—can't I, Azalea?"

The dark handsome face was very earnest, and as it drew nearer to her own, and she looked deep in the eloquent eyes, she could no longer fail to understand.

"What,—what,—" she murmured, drawing back in confusion, "what do you mean?"

"Don't you know what I mean, Brownie? Listen, and I will tell you, then. I love you, dear,—I love you." He held her hands in his own and gazed into her face. "I can't tell you when it came or how,—but suddenly—I knew it! I knew I loved you, and should always love you. Tell me,—tell me, Azalea, that you can learn to love me."

"Oh, don't—I can't—"

"Not just at once, dear,—I can't hope for that. But, can't you learn,—can't you try to learn—If I help you? Brownie,—that's all my own name for you,—isn't it, you nutbrown maid! Brownie, darling,—you *must* love me. I can't bear it if you don't!"

Azalea looked mystified,—then amazed,—and then her face lighted up with a sudden radiant happiness,—she seemed glorified, exalted.

Van Reypen caught her in his arms.

"You do love me,—you witch! you beauty! Azalea, you look transfigured! You *do* love me,—tell me so!"

Then her face changed. She repulsed him,—she sought to leave his encircling clasp.

"Don't!" she cried, "don't! It is horrible!"

She burst into uncontrollable tears, and her whole frame shook with her turbulent sorrow.

"Have I been too abrupt?" asked Van Reypen, filled with dismay. "Give me a little hope, dear, just say you'll let me tell you this some other time, and I'll not trouble you now."

Carolyn Wells

"Oh, it isn't *that*," Azalea sobbed, "it's—oh, *no*! I *can't* tell you,—it's too *dreadful*! Let me go!" and she ran from him and hurried back to the house and up to her own room.

CHAPTER XVII

PHILIP'S REQUEST

"Give me a few minutes of your valuable time all to myself, will you, old chap?" Phil said to Farnsworth, as the two men met in the hall just before the dinner hour.

"Take all you want, I've lots of it," returned the other, cheerily. "Want to borrow a fiver?"

"No; I'm still able to make both ends meet. But, seriously, Bill," as the two men entered Farnsworth's den, and closed the door, "I'm hard hit."

"That sounds as if you were in love,—but I can't think you mean that,—so I wisely opine you've been hit by the fall in Golconda Mining Stock."

"Your wise opinings are 'way off,—but your first suspicion was nearer the mark."

"In love? Good for you, old Phil! Of course it's Elise!"

"Of course it isn't! Had Elise been my fate, I'd have known it long ago."

"Who then? Betty Gale?"

"Wrong again. And blind, too. It's Azalea."

Carolyn Wells

Farnsworth sank limply into a chair. He pretended to be dazed almost to insensibility, and as a matter of fact his surprise was nearly as great as his demonstration of it.

"Azalea!" he gasped. "Our Azalea!"

"Exactly; don't act as if I had suggested the Queen of Sheba! I know what a superior girl she is,—and I know I've not much to recommend me—"

"Oh, Phil,—oh, Van Reypen, stop! Have you lost your senses?"

"I think *you* have!" Phil looked decidedly annoyed. "I must say, Farnsworth, I don't quite get you."

"I beg your pardon, dear old chap, I—I was a bit astounded. You see—"

"I see that I've a right to care for the girl if I choose, and as you are her nearest relative, that I know of, I come to you for sanction of my suit. Aside from your rather inexplicable astonishment—have you any real objection to me as a new cousin-in-law?"

"No! You know I haven't!" Farnsworth held out a cordial hand which the other grasped. "In fact, I think it's fine,—a most admirable arrangement. What *will* Patty say?"

"I hope she'll be pleased. It's no secret that I adored Patty and tried my best to cut you out,—but, not having succeeded in that, I've been glad to be the friend of both of you, and we've had lots of good times, all together. But,—well, I never expected to know another real whole-hearted love,—and then along comes this splendid girl,—this daughter of your own big, beautiful, breezy West, and before I know it, she has taken my heart by storm!"

"But, Phil,—you—you don't know Azalea—"

"I know enough. If you mean her escapades with the picture people or her innocent joke about the patchwork sampler,—I don't care about those little things. She has a wonderful big, noble nature, that will respond quickly to loving care and gentle advice. And,—I *think* she cares for me, but—"

"Of course she cares for you! What girl wouldn't! Don't underestimate yourself or your attractions, Phil. But I'll speak plainly; you're a big man in lots of ways,—beside physically. You're an aristocrat,—of an old family,—and you're very rich. Now,—Azalea—"

"Please don't talk of my birth or wealth as assets. I offer Azalea a heart full of love, and a constant care for her happiness and well-being. If she does care for me, I want your permission to try to win her. I have broached the subject—"

"What did she say?"

"She—oh, I don't know,—she said—well, she ran away!"

"Surprised and a little shy, probably," Farnsworth looked thoughtful. "I may as well tell you, Phil, oh hang it! How shall I put it? Well, there's something queer about Azalea."

"What do you mean,—queer?"

"I don't know. And it may be nothing. But,—her only near relative, so far as I know, is her father. A man I knew years ago,—a cousin of mine,—and a decent, hard-working, plain man. Now, Zaly has not had a single letter from him since she has been here."

"Why? Where is he?"

"I don't know. She won't tell. I've written to him twice,—but I've had no reply. I'm telling you all I know."

"Thank you for being so straightforward. Do you—do you

think there's anything dishonourable—"

"That he's in jail? That's the idea that haunts my brain. I can't think of any other explanation for his continued silence,—and for Azalea's mysterious disinclination to talk about him. Why, Phil, she forged a letter,—wrote one to herself,—and pretended to me that it was from her father!"

"Poor child! How unhappy she must be over it. If she cares for me, Bill, I'll take all that load off her poor little shoulders. I'll get her to tell me the truth, and then we'll see what can be done. But, in any case, or whatever her father may be, it won't affect my love for the girl herself. My idea of birth and breeding is that it gives one an opportunity to be tolerant and generous toward others of fewer advantages. To me, Azalea stands alone,—her family connections, whatever they may be, I accept gladly, for her dear sake."

"I say, Phil, forgive me if I express unwelcome surprise, but—why, you haven't *seemed* to be so deeply interested in Azalea—"

"I know; it *is* pretty sudden. But, she somehow bowled me over all at once. Her brave attitude to-day, when she told her little story, her sweet acceptance of Elise's remarks, made in petty spite, and her whole big spirit of fearless determination to go into the picture work,—only to have it spoiled entirely by the wicked acts of that villain Merritt,—I tell you, Farnsworth, she's a girl of a thousand! I read her, I understand her better than you do, and I see far beneath her untaught, outward manner the real girl,—the sterling traits of a fine character."

"All right, Phil, go in and win! You have my blessing,—and when Patty revives from her first shock of surprise, she'll bless you, too. It was Patty's work, getting Azalea here,—and Patty has tried every way in the world to help and improve her—"

"Patty has done wonders. And has paved the way, I admit. But it is nothing to what I shall do with and for Azalea, when I have her all to myself."

"She's not so very tractable—Zaly has a will of her own."

"She'd not be herself, if she hadn't. That's part of her big nobility of soul. But I'll take care of her manners and customs. If only she'll accept me, I've no fears for the future."

"But you must find out about her father. It's queer that she acts so mysterious about him. And, so far as I know, she's had no letters from anybody back home,—her home is at Horner's Corners. Awful place!"

"If we don't like the place, we'll buy it and make it over," said Van Reypen, serenely. "All right, Farnsworth, you've made me satisfied that I may try to win my prize,—and the rest will follow."

The two men went out to join the others on the porch. Both were in thoughtful mood. Van Reypen full of his new happiness, and eager to see Azalea again, Farnsworth still amazed, and a little uncomfortable over the whole matter. He felt a responsibility for Azalea, and yet, if Phil was willing to take her without further knowledge of her family,—why should he, Bill, object?

Azalea had not yet come downstairs, and Patty chaffed the two men on their sober faces.

"What's the matter?" she cried, gaily. "You two been quarrelling?"

"Come for a stroll on the terrace, and I'll tell you, Patty," said Phil, for he really wanted to tell Patty himself.

"You see," he said, as they passed out of earshot of the others, "I'm bowled over."

"I know! Betty Gale. And I'm *so* glad, Phil. I know you used to like me,—and I was and am fond of you,—but you needn't think I resent your loving another. I'm honestly glad, and I wish you all the happiness in the world!"

"Thank you, Patty, but,—wait a minute."

"Oh, I can't! I'm so excited over it! I'm going to announce it at dinner,—I wonder if I can't get the table re-decorated—with white flowers! I love an announcement party—"

"Patty,—don't,—let me tell you—"

"Oh, I know *you'd* hate the fuss and feathers, but Betty'll love it and—"

"But it *isn't* Betty!" Van Reypen managed to get in.

"Not Betty!" Patty stopped short and turned to face him. "Oh, —Phil,—Elise?"

"You've one more guess coming," he smiled.

"Oh, who? Somebody in New York? Where is she? I'll invite her here!"

"You needn't,—she's here already. Why, Patty, it's Azalea."

"Azalea!" Patty's surprise was greater than Bill's had been, and she stood looking at Van Reypen with an absolutely incredulous gaze.

"Azalea!" she said, again.

"Yes,—and I want you to help me. When I spoke to her, this afternoon, she—she acted—well, strange—"

"Oh, Phil, it was only because she was so surprised,—as I am,—as everybody will be! Imagine Elise!"

Patty's face of horror, that changed to a mischievous smile, annoyed Van Reypen.

"I don't see, Patty, why you take it like that. Bill did, too. Now, it seems to me, if I see noble traits and qualities in Azalea, you and Bill ought to have perception enough to see them too."

"It isn't that,—she has noble traits,—some,—but—oh, Phil, —you and Azalea! King Cophetua and the Beggar Maid!"

"Patty, stop! I won't let you talk like that! I admit I'm blind to her faults,—if she has any,—for I'm desperately in love,—but I do look to you and Bill for sympathy and approval. And I don't want any of that King Cophetua talk, either! Just because I happen to be born under a family tree, and happen to have as much money as I want,—that's no reason for implying that those are my chief attractions. I can give Azalea more worthwhile things than that! I can give her the love and adoration that is every woman's desire and right,—I can give her loving care and help,—I can—"

"Oh, Phil, how splendid you are! You make me 'most wish—" But Patty's honest blue eyes wouldn't let her say the words. "No, I don't wish anything of the sort! You are a splendid man, and I do appreciate you, but I have my Bill, and he's all the world to me. Now, I'm more than glad you've found a your fate at last,—but—Azalea!"

"Stop it, Patty! I find I've got to forbid these repeated expressions of amazement. You *must* get used to the idea, and you may as well begin at once!"

"You're right, and I will! First of all, honest and hearty congratulations and may you both be very, *very* happy,—as happy as we are,—I can't ask more!"

"Thank you, Patty, and will you say a good word for me to Azalea?"

"Why! haven't you asked her yet?"

"Only partly,—that is, she has only partly answered me."

"What did she say?"

"I don't quite know. She was,—well, Patty, she ran away from me."

"Oh, that's all right, then, that's a time-honoured device to postpone the psychological moment! Well, may I make the announcement at dinner?"

"No; I think not. For, though I couldn't help hoping, from the look in her eyes, that she cares for me,—yet she said—"

"What did she say?"

"Nothing coherent or understandable,—but—well, she didn't —she didn't say 'yes'."

"Oh, that's nothing,—she will. But I won't make the announcement till she tells me to. There's the dinner gong,— come on."

It wasn't until the others were seated at the table that Azalea come into the dining-room. She looked quite unlike her usual self, and was very quiet. Her face showed a pathetic, wistful expression, but her eyes were cast down, and now and then the corners of her scarlet mouth trembled.

Patty had arranged that she should sit next Van Reypen, and as Azalea took the place, she found Ray Gale on her other hand.

"'Smatter, Zaly?" he said, merrily, not thinking anything was really troubling her.

"Shell shock," said Van Reypen, to save Azalea the necessity of replying. "She's had a hard day of it, and now she's not to be bothered to talk, if she doesn't want to."

Azalea gave him a grateful look, and under the influence of his gentle kindliness, and mild raillery, she partly recovered her poise, and became almost like her own gay self again.

Much later in the evening, Van Reypen drew her away from the rest and led her to a secluded corner of the great piazza, where he had her alone.

"Now, my princess,—my beloved,—you are to tell me the answer to my plea. Tell me, Azalea,—may I take you to myself? Will you be my very own?"

"I can't say yes, Phil," she replied, softly, the tears gathering in her brown eyes. "I—oh, I thought I could tell you the truth,—but I can't,—I *can't*! I—I love you too much!"

"You've answered me!" cried Van Reypen, his eyes shining with gladness, "if you love me,—nothing else matters! And you can't love me 'too much'! I want all there is of your love,—your dear love! Is it really mine?"

"It's really yours, as far as it's in my power to give it,—but," and Azalea's face grew very sad, "I can't give it to you,—out of consideration of your rights. I can't love you, Philip, I mustn't let myself even think of it!"

"Don't talk nonsense, you blessed child,—you've settled it all when you say you love me! Oh, Azalea, I'm *so* glad, and proud and happy!"

Azalea gave a start as his arms closed round her. "No!" she cried, "no, dear, don't! oh, please don't!"

"Why, darling? Why mayn't I caress my own love,—my promised wife?"

"Oh, no,—I'm not! I can never be your wife! I'm—I'm

not worthy!"

"Hush!" and Van Reypen closed her lips with a tender kiss. "Hush, Azalea, never use the words worthy or unworthy between us. Our love makes us worthy of each other, whatever we may be otherwise."

"Stop,—please stop! Every word you say makes it harder! I can't stand it! It's too dreadful. Let me go,—oh, *please*, let me go!"

Shuddering as with some great fear, Azalea slipped from his arms and ran away. He heard her steps as she went upstairs, and heard a door close,—evidently she had flown to her own room.

Greatly perplexed, Phil went in search of Patty.

"Help me out," he said, in a low tone. "Azalea has gone to her room, and there is certainly something troubling her. Go to her, Patty,—find out what it all means,—and if it is any foolishness about 'unworthiness' or that rubbish, try to make her see that I want her just as she is. I don't care a hang about her ancestors or her father or anything in the whole world, but just Azalea Thorpe!"

Patty looked at his earnest face, and honestly rejoiced that he had found a girl he could care for like that.

"I'll go, Phil," she said, "and I'll bring that young woman to reason! It isn't only coyness,—that isn't Azalea's way,—but she is honestly troubled about something."

But though Patty knocked on Azalea's locked door several times, she heard no response.

"Please let me in, Zaly," she begged, "I just want to talk to you a little."

Still no reply, and then, after exhausting all other arguments, Patty said, "Won't you let me in for Phil's sake? He sent me."

That succeeded, and reluctantly Azalea unlocked the door.

"Don't talk to me, Patty," she pleaded. "I'm in the depths of despair, but you can't help me. Nobody can help me,—and I can't even help myself."

"Who made all this trouble for you?" inquired Patty, casually, her never failing tact instructing her that Azalea would answer that better than protestations of affection.

"I made it myself,—but that doesn't make it any easier to bear."

"Indeed it doesn't," Patty agreed. "But, never mind, Zaly, if you heaped up a mound of trouble, let me help you to pull it down again."

"No; you can't," and Azalea looked at her dully.

"Oh, come now, let me try. Is it about your father?"

Azalea fairly jumped. "What do you mean?"

"Just what I said," returned Patty, calmly. "You know, dear, you've made us think there's something queer about your father. Is he—has he done anything wrong?"

"No, Patty, goodness, gracious no! Mr. Thorpe is a most honoured and honourable man!"

"Now why does she call him Mr. Thorpe?" Patty wondered, but she only said;

"Oh, all right, forgive my suggestion. Why doesn't he write to you?"

"He—he?—oh, Patty, that's the trouble."

"Good! Now we're getting at it. How is that the trouble?"

"Shall I tell you everything?" and poor Azalea looked doubtful as to what to do.

"Yes, dear," Patty said, gently, fearing even yet that an ill-advised word would interrupt or prevent this long-deferred explanation.

"Well, you see,—oh, Patty,—I'm a wicked, deceitful girl—"

"Out with it," urged Patty, not greatly scared by this tragic beginning,—for Azalea was prone to exaggerate.

"I was home, you know, at Horner's Corners—"

A knock on the door was a most unwelcome interruption.

"Don't answer," Patty whispered, "it's Elise,—I heard her step."

But Elise was not so easily rebuffed. "Let me in," she called, "I know you're in there, Azalea,—you and Patty."

Patty went to the door, and opened it slightly. "Go away now, Elise, please," she said, "Azalea and I are having a little confidential chat."

"Not so confidential that I can't be in it too, is it?" and speaking lightly, Elise brushed past Patty and into the room.

"Why, Azalea," she exclaimed, "what *is* the matter? You look like a tragedy queen!"

For Azalea, annoyed at the intrusion, stood, hands clenched, and eyes scowling, and she said angrily, "I don't think people ought to come into other people's rooms, uninvited! I don't call *that* good manners!"

"You're not supposed to know what good manners are," said Elise, giving her a condescending look. "And even if you think you do,—don't try to teach *me!*"

"Oh, Elise," said Patty, reproachfully, "*don't* talk like that! It reflects on you even more than on Zaly."

"Oh, yes, stand up for her,—every one has gone mad over our 'heroine'! I call it disgraceful to be mixed up with that movie concern, and let me tell you, Azalea Thorpe, if you think Mr. Van Reypen is going to overlook or forget that, you're greatly mistaken! You know, Patty,—our Western friend here, is already aspiring toward Philip—"

"Hush, Elise," Patty returned, "better stop before you make a goose of yourself! Phil is aspiring to Azalea's favour, is the truer way to put it!"

"Oh, no, I can't believe that," laughed Elise, "Phil has too much self-respect!"

CHAPTER XVIII

PHILIP'S BROWNIE

At breakfast next morning Azalea's place was vacant.

"I didn't disturb her," said Patty, "for I want her to sleep late, if she can. She is such an active young person, she gets tired, —though she rarely admits it."

And then Janet came in. "Mrs. Farnsworth," she said, "Miss Thorpe is not in her room. Perhaps she has gone for one of her early morning walks. But on her dressing-table I found these two notes."

The maid handed Patty one of the letters and gave the other to Van Reypen. Both were addressed in Azalea's handwriting and the two who took them felt a sudden foreboding as to the contents.

Nor were their fears ill-founded. With an exclamation of dismay, Patty handed hers over to Farnsworth, who read it quickly, and looked at his wife with a serious face.

"Poor little Azalea," he said, "what *can* it all mean?"

For the note read:

DEAR PATTY:

I'm a wicked girl, and I can't impose on you any longer. I am going away. Don't try to find me,—just forget me. I love you all,—but I have no right to be among good people.

AZALEA.

"What's in yours, Phil?" Farnsworth asked, and Van Reypen handed it to him without a word.

MY DEAR MR. VAN REYPEN:

I can't go away without leaving a word for you. But it is only to say, please forget the girl who calls herself

AZALEA.

Then the notes were shown to the other two guests, Elise and Channing, for the departure of Azalea could not be kept secret, and of course they must immediately put forth every possible effort to find her.

"I always thought she was queer," said Elise, "but these notes are the queerest thing yet! Do you suppose she has eloped?"

"Hush, Elise," said Farnsworth, sternly. "I know you don't like Azalea, but I must ask you not to talk against her while you are under my roof. Whatever she is, she is my kin,—and I shall start at once in search of her, and learn the secret,—the mystery of her life. She *has* acted 'queer,' I freely admit it, but I, for one, believe she is all right and whatever is troubling her is not her fault or wrong-doing."

"Good for you, old man!" cried Philip, "I'm with you in your search. We'll find her, of course. First, we must find out where she went."

This statement was so obvious and uttered so earnestly that Patty laughed.

"True, Mr. Sherlock Holmes," she said. "And just how shall we set about it?"

But Phil didn't laugh,—he answered her question seriously.

"First, Patty, you must question the servants, and see if any one saw her go. You know, she must have gone early this morning,—she couldn't have gone off in the night."

The result of the inquiry was that the cook, who was around early, had seen Azalea start away from the house at about six o'clock. She had not thought it strange at all, for Azalea often went for a long walk before breakfast. Cook said that Azalea wore a travelling suit and carried a fair-sized bag.

"So far, so good," said Phil; "next, Patty, will you go and look round her room? See what she took with her,—and see if she left any more notes."

"No notes," Patty said, on her return from this errand. "But she took all her jewellery and money, a house dress and a few toilet things. Janet and I could easily tell what was missing."

"Now," said Farnsworth, "first, *why* did she go, and second, *where* would she be likely to go?"

"Never mind the why and wherefore," returned Phil, "but, as you say, where would she probably go? Not over to the Gales', of course, that's too near home. I am ready to declare that she went to the moving-picture studios."

"Of course she did!" agreed Elise; "I think she's in love with that Merritt person—"

"Nonsense, Elise," laughed Channing; "she loves that man like a cat loves hot soap! I know better than that. But I think she may have gone over there to see Mrs. Bixby. That woman has been kind to Azalea, and I feel sure that's where she'd go."

"Then that's where *I* go," stated Van Reypen, rising from the table. "I daresay you're right, Chick. May I take the little roadster, Bill, and whiz over there and bring her back?"

"Go ahead, boy, and good luck to you."

But Farnsworth was not at all sanguine as to the bringing back of Azalea. He knew her, in some ways, far better than Van Reypen did, and he felt sure that when Azalea decided to go away, she would not be easily found.

But Van Reypen started cheerily off and went to the studios.

There he was met by blank disappointment. Mrs. Bixby was greatly interested in his story, and greatly concerned for Azalea's welfare, but she declared the girl had not come there.

Van Reypen was not quite sure she was telling him the truth, but his deep anxiety so stirred the motherly heart of Mrs. Bixby that she assured him earnestly that her statements were absolutely true, and that she was as anxious to find the missing girl as her friends were.

But she could offer no suggestion as to any way to look, and poor Philip went back, disheartened and disappointed.

All the morning they searched the grounds and the neighbourhood; they ransacked Azalea's belongings in hope of some old letter or clue of some sort. But nothing gave so much as a hint of anything that could have happened to her, that made her go away.

"I believe it's all your fault, Elise," said Van Reypen, angrily, for his alarm and sorrow made him forget his usual courtesy. "You've never liked Azalea, and you said mean things to her!"

"Now, Phil," remonstrated Patty, "don't talk like that. Elise and Azalea were not congenial, but Elise wouldn't do anything to make Azalea run away, and Azalea wouldn't run, if she did!"

This involved speech brought a laugh, but Philip went on; "I think she would. Azalea is more sensitive than you thought her. None of you understand her,—well, except Patty,—and her poor little heart was broken by your criticisms and continual reproofs. Suppose she isn't quite as well up in the airs and graces of society as you all are,—she has other traits that make up for that—"

"Oh, Philip, you're hopelessly in love with her!" and Elise laughed jeeringly.

"I am in love with her," he returned, "and I make no secret of it. But not hopelessly, Elise. I shall find her,—I don't know how or where, but I never will give up the quest until I succeed!"

"Good for you," cried Patty, "that's the way to talk! I'll help, —and though there's not any apparent way to look just now, —we'll find one."

It was about noon when Van Reypen was called to the telephone.

A strange but pleasant voice spoke to him, and asked him if he knew Alice Adams.

"No, I don't," said Phil, wonderingly.

"She knows you, and—well, I may be doing the wrong thing, but I wish you could come here."

"Where, please? and why should I come? I don't know Miss Adams,—I'm sure."

"She is a dark-haired girl, with big, brown eyes, and a Western way of speaking—"

"What? Has *she* just come to you? Does she wear a tan-coloured cloth suit,—and a hat with coque feathers?"

"Yes, she does! *Now* will you come?"

"Where? Who are you?—I mean, may I ask your name?"

"I am Miss Grayson,—a motion-picture actress—"

"Yes, yes,—where are you? Where shall I come?"

"To my home in New York City." She gave him the address. "You see, Miss Adams came here because she knows Miss Frawley,—we live together—but Miss Frawley is out of town,—and I persuaded Miss Adams to stay with me until her return. I can't make out the trouble, but I have learned the address of the Farnsworths and—oh, well, I may as well tell you, Miss Adams talked in her sleep. She arrived here utterly exhausted, and on the verge of nervous prostration. But, it may be, some sleep will set her nerves right, if the cause of the trouble can be removed. And,—I know I am intruding,—but I can't help thinking that it's a lovers' quarrel, and *you* can set it right!"

"You've guessed only part of it, Miss Grayson. It isn't a lovers' quarrel,—exactly,—but I *can* set it right! Will you promise to keep Miss—Adams there, until I can get there?"

"Yes, indeed. She's asleep yet,—but it's a broken slumber, and she murmurs constantly of you,—and of her other friends."

"Thank you a thousand times, I'll be there in an hour. Good-bye."

"Come along, Patty," Van Reypen cried, as he hung up the receiver, "come on, Bill! I've found her! She's assumed the name of Alice Adams,—and she's with a sweet-voiced lady named Grayson. Come on,—I'll tell you the rest as we go."

They didn't break the speed laws, as their car flew down to New York, but it was only because that would have meant delay in reaching their goal. About mid-afternoon they arrived at Miss Grayson's apartment and surprised Azalea by entering the room where she sat.

"You naughty girl!" cried Patty,—but as she noted Azalea's pale face and worried, harassed eyes, she just clasped her in her arms, with a little crooning murmur of affection.

"It's all right, whatever it is," she reassured, for Azalea turned big, frightened eyes on Farnsworth.

"You bet it's all right!" Philip cried, as he stepped eagerly forward.

With a tired little sigh, Azalea put her hand in his. "How did you find me?" she began, but Van Reypen said, "Never mind that, now. You just come back home with us,—and first thank Miss Grayson prettily for her kindness to you."

Miss Grayson, a pretty, round-faced girl, was greatly interested in the dramatic situation, and though she disclaimed any occasion for thanks, yet she very much wanted to know what it was all about.

"I already like Miss Adams too well to let her go entirely out of my life," she said, with spirit. "I claim my right to know a little about it."

"It *is* your right," said Farnsworth, "and first of all this runaway of ours is not Miss Adams, but Miss Thorpe."

"No," said Azalea, with an air of decision, "I'm *not* Miss Thorpe,—and I *am* Alice Adams."

"Flighty," said Farnsworth, "and no wonder. She's been under a good deal of nervous strain lately."

"No; I'm not flighty," persisted Azalea, who was entirely composed now, and who spoke firmly, though she was evidently controlling herself with an effort.

"And I'm going to confess now," she went on. "Now and here. Miss Grayson is so kind and dear I don't mind her knowing, and the rest of you *must* know. I must tell you,—I can't *live* if I don't."

"All right, Zaly, dear, tell us," and Patty sat beside her, and put a caressing hand on her arm.

"I am Alice Adams," Azalea said, "and I am not Azalea Thorpe at all,—and I never was."

"Oh!" said Farnsworth, beginning to see light.

"I am a wicked girl," the pathetic little voice went on. "I lived in Homer's Corners,—and I lived with the woman who keeps the post-office there. I've been an orphan since I was four, and this woman brought me up,—though it scarcely could be called that, for she only looked on me as her assistant in the office and in her house.

"Well, one day a letter came for Azalea Thorpe. Now, the Thorpes moved away from Horner's Corners two years ago, and we never knew their new address. The few letters that came for them were sent to the Dead Letter Office. This one would have been, but for the fact that it was unsealed.

"It had been sealed, but the envelope was all unstuck, and—I read the letter. I own up to it,—I know it was wrong,—but I didn't know then *how* wrong. You see, I wasn't taught much about honour and right. It is only since I have been with good people that I realise what an awful thing I did. When I read it, I couldn't help thinking what a pity for that wonderful invitation to her to make a visit in the East, to be wasted! And the more I thought, the more I was possessed of an idea that I might personate Azalea Thorpe and have the visit myself. Oh, if you *knew* how I hated the place where I lived,—how I hated the home I had,—how I wanted to get out into the great world, and have my chance! And, yes, I wanted to be a moving-picture actress. I was *sure* I could do better than the pictures I saw in that little town, and—well, the more I thought about it,—the more it seemed an easy and plausible thing to do.

"I did it. I answered Patty's letter as if I were really Azalea Thorpe,—you see, I had known her all my life, until she moved away, and then I packed up my things and came East, resolved to pretend I *was* Azalea and see what happened. It didn't seem so dreadful—I thought at first, it was just a big lark,—but now,—oh, *now* I know how right and honourable people look on a thing like that!"

She cast a hopeless glance at Van Reypen, and though he smiled at her and started toward her she shook her head and waved him back.

"On the trip East, I met the Bixbys, and as we at once arranged for my entrance into their studios, I was more than ever eager to put the matter through.

"So I came. Oh, I hate to think how I imposed on the Farnsworths! They were *so* kind to me, right from the start. Then they asked me questions about my father, and I didn't know what to do or say. I tried to fool you, Bill, with a made-up letter but I didn't succeed. And,—all the way along, I kept feeling worse and worse,—meaner and meaner—at the life of deceit I was leading. I made good in the pictures,—and oh, Patty, will you *ever* forgive me for taking Baby over there! But I knew she was safe with me, and, like all the rest, I didn't realise how bad I was!

"I don't ask or expect forgiveness,—I know you couldn't grant *that*. But lately I felt I couldn't go on any longer,—and I couldn't bring myself to confess,—so,—I ran away."

"And you are really Alice Adams?" asked Farnsworth, but Phil interrupted.

"Wait a minute, everybody. Before Azalea—or Alice,—or

whoever she is, says another word, I want to say that she is my promised wife! I want you, dear, and whatever your name is, I want it to be changed to Van Reypen. Tell me,—tell them all,—that you consent."

A beautiful expression came over the girl's face.

She turned to Philip, her soft, dark eyes shining with utter joy and a tender smile of glad surprise curving her quivering lips.

"Oh," she breathed, "oh, *Phil*!"

"You *do* consent?" he urged, "you must say yes, before you tell us any more!"

"May I, Patty?" and a shy, sweet face looked questioningly at the one she was glad to consider her mentor.

"I think so," Patty smiled back, for she knew how matters stood with Phil, and she had faith in the true heart of the girl beside her.

"Yes, then," she said, softly, looking at Philip,—and that was their troth-plight.

"Go on, dear," he said, briefly, and with a glad smile in his eyes.

"There's little more to tell; I am Alice Adams, and my father was born in Boston—"

"Good gracious, Phil!" Patty cried. "Why, this child is a real Adams!"

"Of course she is," said Farnsworth, "I knew the Adamses that lived in Horner's Corners. You see, I was there some years myself. Why, your mother was a sweet little woman, with a face like Dresden china."

"Yes; I've a miniature of her. She was beautiful. I'm like my father—"

"And *you're* beautiful!" cried Patty, kissing her. "Oh, Zaly,—I can't call you anything else! what a story you *have* told us!"

"And now, let's proceed to forget it," said Farnsworth, in his big, genial way. "You and I'll talk it over a little when we're alone,—but just now, I adopt you as my cousin,—I'm proud to have an Adams in my family, even if only by adoption! Your escapade was a wild one,—er—Alice,—but it was an *escapade*, —not a crime. And for my part, you are fully and freely forgiven, and—here's where Patty takes up the theme."

"I do," said Patty; "and I add my full and free forgiveness to Little Billee's and I invite you to come right back to Wistaria Porch and make us a long visit,—as Alice Adams."

"And we thank *you*, Miss Grayson," Farnsworth said, "for restoring our lost cousin, and at the same time giving us a new one!"

Miss Grayson laughed. "It's been a perfect show for me," she said; "I think it's all more dramatic than any play I ever acted in."

"Come, Alice, dear," Van Reypen said, with an air of proprietorship, "where's your coat?"

Shyly, Alice looked up at him.

"Are you sure you want me?" she said.

"Sure I want an Adams? Well, rather! I never aspired to such a renowned name for my *fiancee*! My own family pride is humbled to the dust."

"Nonsense!" laughed Patty, "the Van Reypen stock can hold its own!"

And then they quickly got ready and started for home.

Farnsworth took the wheel, and invited Patty to sit beside him.

This left Van Reypen and Alice together in the tonneau, and neither objected to the arrangement.

They conversed softly as the car sped swiftly along, and Phil realised how beautiful was the dear face beside him, now that worry and care had been replaced by happiness and love.

"But I don't see how you *can* forgive me," Alice said, "I did such a *dreadful* thing."

"I forgive you for two reasons," Van Reypen returned, "first, because you didn't appreciate the real *wrong* you were doing, and second, because I *love* you. Love you enough to forgive far more than that!"

"You'll never have to forgive me for anything again, for I'm never going to do anything you'll disapprove of. I'm among nice people forever now,—and I'm going to learn to be like them."

"You're one of the 'nice people' yourself, by birth, and your name is among the best. But I doubt if I can learn to call you 'Alice.' To me, you will always be 'Brownie',—my own Brownie girl."

"I like that best," she said, contentedly, and smiled happily at Philip as his hand clasped hers, and his eyes carried a message of love that needed no spoken word to tell of its depth and sincerity.

Choose from Thousands of 1stWorldLibrary Classics By

A. M. Barnard
Ada Leverson
Adolphus William Ward
Aesop
Agatha Christie
Alexander Aaronsohn
Alexander Kielland
Alexandre Dumas
Alfred Gatty
Alfred Ollivant
Alice Duer Miller
Alice Turner Curtis
Alice Dunbar
Allen Chapman
Alleyne Ireland
Ambrose Bierce
Amelia E. Barr
Amory H. Bradford
Andrew Lang
Andrew McFarland Davis
Andy Adams
Angela Brazil
Anna Alice Chapin
Anna Sewell
Annie Besant
Annie Hamilton Donnell
Annie Payson Call
Annie Roe Carr
Annonaymous
Anton Chekhov
Archibald Lee Fletcher
Arnold Bennett
Arthur C. Benson
Arthur Conan Doyle
Arthur M. Winfield
Arthur Ransome
Arthur Schnitzler
Arthur Train
Atticus
B.H. Baden-Powell
B. M. Bower
B. C. Chatterjee
Baroness Emmuska Orczy
Baroness Orczy
Basil King
Bayard Taylor
Ben Macomber
Bertha Muzzy Bower
Bjornstjerne Bjornson

Booth Tarkington
Boyd Cable
Bram Stoker
C. Collodi
C. E. Orr
C. M. Ingleby
Carolyn Wells
Catherine Parr Traill
Charles A. Eastman
Charles Amory Beach
Charles Dickens
Charles Dudley Warner
Charles Farrar Browne
Charles Ives
Charles Kingsley
Charles Klein
Charles Hanson Towne
Charles Lathrop Pack
Charles Romyn Dake
Charles Whibley
Charles Willing Beale
Charlotte M. Braeme
Charlotte M. Yonge
Charlotte Perkins Stetson
Clair W. Hayes
Clarence Day Jr.
Clarence E. Mulford
Clemence Housman
Confucius
Coningsby Dawson
Cornelis DeWitt Wilcox
Cyril Burleigh
D. H. Lawrence
Daniel Defoe
David Garnett
Dinah Craik
Don Carlos Janes
Donald Keyhoe
Dorothy Kilner
Dougan Clark
Douglas Fairbanks
E. Nesbit
E. P. Roe
E. Phillips Oppenheim
E. S. Brooks
Earl Barnes
Edgar Rice Burroughs
Edith Van Dyne
Edith Wharton

Edward Everett Hale
Edward J. O'Biren
Edward S. Ellis
Edwin L. Arnold
Eleanor Atkins
Eleanor Hallowell Abbott
Eliot Gregory
Elizabeth Gaskell
Elizabeth McCracken
Elizabeth Von Arnim
Ellem Key
Emerson Hough
Emilie F. Carlen
Emily Bronte
Emily Dickinson
Enid Bagnold
Enilor Macartney Lane
Erasmus W. Jones
Ernie Howard Pie
Ethel May Dell
Ethel Turner
Ethel Watts Mumford
Eugene Sue
Eugenie Foa
Eugene Wood
Eustace Hale Ball
Evelyn Everett-green
Everard Cotes
F. H. Cheley
F. J. Cross
F. Marion Crawford
Fannie E. Newberry
Federick Austin Ogg
Ferdinand Ossendowski
Fergus Hume
Florence A. Kilpatrick
Fremont B. Deering
Francis Bacon
Francis Darwin
Frances Hodgson Burnett
Frances Parkinson Keyes
Frank Gee Patchin
Frank Harris
Frank Jewett Mather
Frank L. Packard
Frank V. Webster
Frederic Stewart Isham
Frederick Trevor Hill
Frederick Winslow Taylor

Friedrich Kerst
Friedrich Nietzsche
Fyodor Dostoyevsky
G.A. Henty
G.K. Chesterton
Gabrielle E. Jackson
Garrett P. Serviss
Gaston Leroux
George A. Warren
George Ade
Geroge Bernard Shaw
George Cary Eggleston
George Durston
George Ebers
George Eliot
George Gissing
George MacDonald
George Meredith
George Orwell
George Sylvester Viereck
George Tucker
George W. Cable
George Wharton James
Gertrude Atherton
Gordon Casserly
Grace E. King
Grace Gallatin
Grace Greenwood
Grant Allen
Guillermo A. Sherwell
Gulielma Zollinger
Gustav Flaubert
H. A. Cody
H. B. Irving
H.C. Bailey
H. G. Wells
H. H. Munro
H. Irving Hancock
H. R. Naylor
H. Rider Haggard
H. W. C. Davis
Haldeman Julius
Hall Caine
Hamilton Wright Mabie
Hans Christian Andersen
Harold Avery
Harold McGrath
Harriet Beecher Stowe
Harry Castlemon
Harry Coghill
Harry Houidini

Hayden Carruth
Helent Hunt Jackson
Helen Nicolay
Hendrik Conscience
Hendy David Thoreau
Henri Barbusse
Henrik Ibsen
Henry Adams
Henry Ford
Henry Frost
Henry James
Henry Jones Ford
Henry Seton Merriman
Henry W Longfellow
Herbert A. Giles
Herbert Carter
Herbert N. Casson
Herman Hesse
Hildegard G. Frey
Homer
Honore De Balzac
Horace B. Day
Horace Walpole
Horatio Alger Jr.
Howard Pyle
Howard R. Garis
Hugh Lofting
Hugh Walpole
Humphry Ward
Ian Maclaren
Inez Haynes Gillmore
Irving Bacheller
Isabel Cecilia Williams
Isabel Hornibrook
Israel Abrahams
Ivan Turgenev
J.G.Austin
J. Henri Fabre
J. M. Barrie
J. M. Walsh
J. Macdonald Oxley
J. R. Miller
J. S. Fletcher
J. S. Knowles
J. Storer Clouston
J. W. Duffield
Jack London
Jacob Abbott
James Allen
James Andrews
James Baldwin

James Branch Cabell
James DeMille
James Joyce
James Lane Allen
James Lane Allen
James Oliver Curwood
James Oppenheim
James Otis
James R. Driscoll
Jane Abbott
Jane Austen
Jane L. Stewart
Janet Aldridge
Jens Peter Jacobsen
Jerome K. Jerome
Jessie Graham Flower
John Buchan
John Burroughs
John Cournos
John F. Kennedy
John Gay
John Glasworthy
John Habberton
John Joy Bell
John Kendrick Bangs
John Milton
John Philip Sousa
John Taintor Foote
Jonas Lauritz Idemil Lie
Jonathan Swift
Joseph A. Altsheler
Joseph Carey
Joseph Conrad
Joseph E. Badger Jr
Joseph Hergesheimer
Joseph Jacobs
Jules Vernes
Julian Hawthrone
Julie A Lippmann
Justin Huntly McCarthy
Kakuzo Okakura
Karle Wilson Baker
Kate Chopin
Kenneth Grahame
Kenneth McGaffey
Kate Langley Bosher
Kate Langley Bosher
Katherine Cecil Thurston
Katherine Stokes
L. A. Abbot
L. T. Meade

L. Frank Baum
Latta Griswold
Laura Dent Crane
Laura Lee Hope
Laurence Housman
Lawrence Beasley
Leo Tolstoy
Leonid Andreyev
Lewis Carroll
Lewis Sperry Chafer
Lilian Bell
Lloyd Osbourne
Louis Hughes
Louis Joseph Vance
Louis Tracy
Louisa May Alcott
Lucy Fitch Perkins
Lucy Maud Montgomery
Luther Benson
Lydia Miller Middleton
Lyndon Orr
M. Corvus
M. H. Adams
Margaret E. Sangster
Margret Howth
Margaret Vandercook
Margaret W. Hungerford
Margret Penrose
Maria Edgeworth
Maria Thompson Daviess
Mariano Azuela
Marion Polk Angellotti
Mark Overton
Mark Twain
Mary Austin
Mary Catherine Crowley
Mary Cole
Mary Hastings Bradley
Mary Roberts Rinehart
Mary Rowlandson
M. Wollstonecraft Shelley
Maud Lindsay
Max Beerbohm
Myra Kelly
Nathaniel Hawthrone
Nicolo Machiavelli
O. F. Walton
Oscar Wilde

Owen Johnson
P.G. Wodehouse
Paul and Mabel Thorne
Paul G. Tomlinson
Paul Severing
Percy Brebner
Percy Keese Fitzhugh
Peter B. Kyne
Plato
Quincy Allen
R. Derby Holmes
R. L. Stevenson
R. S. Ball
Rabindranath Tagore
Rahul Alvares
Ralph Bonehill
Ralph Henry Barbour
Ralph Victor
Ralph Waldo Emmerson
Rene Descartes
Ray Cummings
Rex Beach
Rex E. Beach
Richard Harding Davis
Richard Jefferies
Richard Le Gallienne
Robert Barr
Robert Frost
Robert Gordon Anderson
Robert L. Drake
Robert Lansing
Robert Lynd
Robert Michael Ballantyne
Robert W. Chambers
Rosa Nouchette Carey
Rudyard Kipling
Saint Augustine
Samuel B. Allison
Samuel Hopkins Adams
Sarah Bernhardt
Sarah C. Hallowell
Selma Lagerlof
Sherwood Anderson
Sigmund Freud
Standish O'Grady
Stanley Weyman
Stella Benson
Stella M. Francis

Stephen Crane
Stewart Edward White
Stijn Streuvels
Swami Abhedananda
Swami Parmananda
T. S. Ackland
T. S. Arthur
The Princess Der Ling
Thomas A. Janvier
Thomas A Kempis
Thomas Anderton
Thomas Bailey Aldrich
Thomas Bulfinch
Thomas De Quincey
Thomas Dixon
Thomas H. Huxley
Thomas Hardy
Thomas More
Thornton W. Burgess
U. S. Grant
Upton Sinclair
Valentine Williams
Various Authors
Vaughan Kester
Victor Appleton
Victor G. Durham
Victoria Cross
Virginia Woolf
Wadsworth Camp
Walter Camp
Walter Scott
Washington Irving
Wilbur Lawton
Wilkie Collins
Willa Cather
Willard F. Baker
William Dean Howells
William le Queux
W. Makepeace Thackeray
William W. Walter
William Shakespeare
Winston Churchill
Yei Theodora Ozaki
Yogi Ramacharaka
Young E. Allison
Zane Grey

www.ingramcontent.com/pod-product-compliance
Lightning Source LLC
Chambersburg PA
CBHW050041180626
46810CB00002B/843